CURSED ANGEL

DRAGON'S GIFT: THE STORM BOOK 3

VERONICA DOUGLAS
LINSEY HALL

MAGIC SIDE PRESS

For our teachers, old and new.

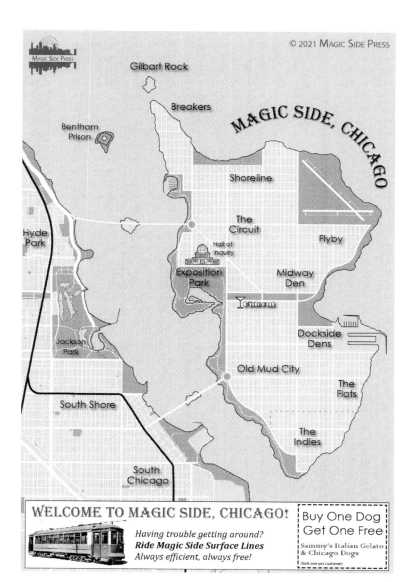

Neve

The ether wrenched my body in a thousand directions and ejected me onto the littered street.

My street. Faebrook Avenue in Old Mud City.

My heart sank as I took in the wreckage caused by the efreet—and *me*—two days ago. The worst of the mess had been cleared away, but workmen were still sweeping up glass and mortar from the street and sidewalks.

Walking past a broken fire hydrant, I recalled the disaster that had unfolded—the firestorm unleashed by the efreet, Amira's portal, Damian. And the hurricane that I had become.

I shuddered.

In that moment, I had focused only on destroying the efreet. In my rage, I'd lost sight of everything else. I'd devastated my neighborhood trying to save it.

I closed my eyes, pushing the memory from my mind.

Amira had magically healed my wounds in the Realm of Water, but my body suddenly felt ragged.

Her and her father had left me with a thousand and one warnings that still rang in my head. *Don't get involved with a FireSoul—they're monsters that kill to steal magic. Find a way to control your powers. And whatever you do, don't grant any wishes.*

She had begged me to stay. Even though Amira and her father were marids—water genies—she said they could help me master my magic and even learn to grant wishes safely.

But I had to return home. I had to make sure Rhiannon was okay, that my city was okay.

Stepping over the trunk of an uprooted tree, I looked up at the blackened brickwork skeleton of my apartment. All of my belongings were destroyed. My memories, my clothes. My books.

I stepped into the wreckage and winced at the crunch of glass and charred keepsakes beneath my feet.

Pushing aside a broken wardrobe, I searched for anything that might have survived the inferno, but everything was charred and damp. A picture frame peeked out beneath a pile of bricks, and I reached down, recognizing it immediately. The glass was shattered, and the photograph blackened, but two smiling faces stared back at me—Rhiannon and me in the Hideout, our go-to bar owned by our friend Diana.

Rhiannon.

I hadn't spoken to her since I'd left for Cairo six days ago. She must have been worried sick, but I'd lost my phone in the desert, and there wasn't reception in the Realm of Water. Panic flared in my chest. We'd defeated the efreet, but the djinn was still out there. It had kidnapped her once, and she could be a target. I needed to find a phone to call her.

"Hey, girl. You okay?" The voice startled me.

I stood and turned, meeting the gaze of a woman in her twenties. Blonde hair, tank top and jeans, smoking a cigarette. Fae, judging by her pointy ears and signature.

She flicked the ash off the end of her cigarette and nodded to my ruined home. "You lived here, huh? What a mess. Can I help?"

"Do you have a cell phone? I need to make a call."

"Sure." She reached into her pocket and handed me her cell.

"Thanks." I unlocked the screen with a quick swipe, then dialed Rhiannon. Her number was one of two I knew by heart. The other was the Hideout.

"Hello?" Rhiannon answered after two rings.

I let out a heavy sigh. "Rhia. Thank fates you're okay."

"Neve! Where have you been? Oh, my gods, I've been so worried. Where are you? I'm coming." Her voice was frantic.

"Sorry. I'll explain everything. I'm at my apartment —well, what *used* to be my apartment."

Rhiannon paused on the line. "I know. I went by yesterday. I'm so sorry. It's going to be okay...you'll stay with me."

"Thanks." I breathed deeply, forcing down the rising sorrow in my throat. The important thing was that Rhiannon was safe. My belongings could be replaced. "Where can we meet?"

"Come to the Hall of Inquiry."

"Not there. We need to talk privately."

I had no idea where I stood with the Order. I had gotten a temporary suspension—as well as a promotion —when I cut work to rescue Rhiannon. If they found out that I was even partially responsible for destroying Faebrook Avenue with my uncontrolled magic, there would be hell to pay.

I could lose my job or get locked up. And there would be a lot of questions—ones I wasn't ready to answer.

"How about our spot near Sammy's? I can be there in fifteen." Rhiannon meant Sammy's Italian Gelato and Chicago Dogs at Exposition Park, where we often met during our lunch breaks.

"See you there." I ended the call and handed the

phone back to the woman. "Thanks again. Do you live here, too?"

"The orange two-story down the block." She stubbed her cigarette out on a brick and stuffed it in her pocket. "Mine isn't so bad, but that doesn't matter."

"What do you mean?"

"Some rich donor—anonymous and all—is rebuilding the whole street." She shrugged. "If you ask me, I think it's the Order. They unleashed that fire storm by accident. Now they're trying to cover it up."

"Hmm. You're probably right." Of course she wasn't, but conspiracy theories were better than the truth—that I'd unleashed a freaking efreet on Magic Side. Not to mention the maelstrom I'd become.

"Just be sure to check in with the MDMA."

She meant the unfortunately named Magical Disaster Management Agency, founded in the 1940s—not the drug.

"There's a stipend to cover your living expenses while all this is rebuilt," the woman continued, gesturing to the dilapidated buildings. "Also from the *anonymous* donor."

I had my own suspicions as to who that was.

Damian Malek.

Just the thought of him was like a blow to the gut.

FireSoul. Betrayer.

This had to be him, and I didn't know what to think.

Nothing was ever direct with Damian. There was always a hidden motive, a second side to the coin.

So he was paying to rebuild the neighborhood using wealth he had stolen, blood money from the Chicago Underworld. Was this some form of atonement? A sign of compassion? Or just another move on a chessboard, furthering his own agenda?

While it brought me comfort that he was taking care of my neighbors, I'd rather sleep on the street than take a penny of his dirty money.

Of course it had to be an *anonymous* donation. He was a compulsive liar and two-faced to his core. Even the good he did was masked in deceit.

How had I ever trusted him?

Amira's warnings burned in my mind: *Never trust a FireSoul.*

I'd never met one before Damian, but I'd heard stories working in the Order. FireSouls were mad with a lust for treasure and power. They would murder you to steal your magic.

Was Damian pretending to care for me just to kill me and take my power? And even if he did care, could he control himself, or would he drain me dry like a blood-crazed vampire?

I had seen it in my dreams, *twice*: Damian had killed me without remorse and stolen my power. My stomach turned as I remembered how it felt to have my magic torn away.

Dreams, or were they premonitions, warnings from the fates themselves?

I needed to stay away from that man and his lies, no matter how pure his intentions seemed.

I walked three blocks and caught a trolley to the Circuit. The seats were largely occupied, and I didn't want to sit next to the vampire in row three who was eying me suspiciously, so I stood next to a woman with pink hair. My temper was still hot, but the thought of seeing Rhia cooled me down.

After ten minutes, I hopped off at 56th Street. Skirting the Hall of Inquiry, I picked up the pace when I recognized two detectives leaving the building. I didn't know them personally, but they used to bully me when I was a researcher in the Order's Archives, and I was probably on their wanted list after what had unfolded at my apartment.

If they knew.

Best to avoid them.

I'd have to check in with the Order soon. Explain things to my boss, Gretchen. But I wanted to speak with Rhiannon first. I needed to get the lay of the land, and I had a lot to get off my chest—things I *couldn't* tell the Order.

My hand went for my missing cell phone for the umpteenth time. I felt naked without it and my khanjar.

Judging from the position of the sun, it must have been close to ten a.m. as I slipped into Exposition Park, the living remnant of Chicago's 1893 World's Fair. Though parts of it had changed, much of it was the same, with several grand pavilions, a museum by the lake, amusement park rides, and idle pushcart vendors everywhere.

The park wasn't busy at this hour, and I spotted Rhiannon in front of Sammy's famous food truck. She was decked out in an embroidered cotton jacket, black jeans, and some mean cowboy boots. As if sensing me, she turned. "There you are!"

We hugged, and I had to pry her arms from me.

"You have to tell me everything. But first"—she turned and grabbed two Chicago dogs and a giant cup of lemon gelato from the takeout window of Sammy's— "I ordered your favorite."

It was a little early for lunch, but I was starving. I took the Chicago dog and dug into the gelato, its tangy sweetness reviving my spirits. "You're the best, Rhia."

I waved at Sammy, who popped his head out of the window. His eyes glowed orange like a furnace, and he smiled, his hands occupied with four gelato cups. I hadn't yet figured out what species Sammy was, but his gelato and Chicago dogs were the bomb.

We walked to a bench overlooking a pond dotted with water lilies and sat. Rhiannon waited until we'd nearly finished our dogs before turning to me. "Spill it. I can't wait any longer. Where the hell have you been this past week?"

I spent the next twenty minutes telling her everything—Helwan, Matthias's betrayal, Amira, the efreet, and Damian being a FireSoul. A weight was lifted off my shoulders, but the ache in my chest was still there.

"Holy hell, you've been busy," Rhiannon said. "And Damian. Fates. I knew there was a darkness to him, but a *FireSoul*?"

"Yup. My life is a mess." I sighed. "But first things first, I need to find Matthias and figure out what he's up to."

"I hate to say it, but I think you need to tell Gretchen —about Matthias, at least."

I knew it was true, and though I'd probably get reprimanded again, a part of me felt relieved. Now that it was just me, this burden was too heavy to bear alone. I looked over at her. "Will you come with me when I go in?"

Rhiannon smiled and gave my hand a light squeeze. "Of course. I've always got your back."

Maybe things weren't so bad.

I was home with Rhia, and the sky was bright. I leaned back, feeling the sunshine warm my face, enjoying a brief reprieve from the stress of it all.

"Speaking of which!" Rhiannon sat upright and reached into her purse. "Here, I picked this up for you. Your number is the same, and all of your contacts should be on there."

She handed me a sleek black cell phone.

"How did you know?" I asked, shocked. She'd also loaded my favorite wallpaper, too—a picture of Elvis, Rhia's fat cat.

"I figured you lost it when you called me on that wack number. Plus, your phone has been going to voicemail for days."

I hugged her. "Thanks, Rhia. You're seriously the best."

"I'm just glad you're back and safe. Also"—she unzipped her cotton jacket and handed it to me with a wink—"Your tattoos are wicked, but I think you should keep them under wraps."

"Good point." With everything going on, I'd completely forgotten about the white tattoos that now snaked up my arm and much of my chest. The tank top I was wearing made them all too obvious.

Rhia suddenly froze, her face focused on something behind my right shoulder.

The hair on my neck stood on end, and I spun, half expecting to see the djinn or Matthias. Instead, a tiny glowing dragon hovered behind me, flapping its wings.

"Spark! You're alive." Joy flooded me, and I reached out my hand. I hadn't seen him since we left the Realm of Fire.

The little dragon landed on my outstretched fingers and nuzzled my palm with his nose.

"Rhia, this is Spark, my familiar. Spark, Rhia." I gestured to Rhiannon, who was staring at me blankly.

"You have a *dragon* familiar?" she replied, astonishment pulling at her words.

"He's actually a fire sprite, but he likes to pretend he's a dragon. He's been with me since my first planeswalk as a kid. He hasn't been able to fully appear until recently."

Spark hopped onto Rhiannon's shoulder and began nibbling on her neck.

"That tickles!" She laughed as he disappeared beneath her shoulder-length blonde hair.

I like her. She smells good, Spark said.

"I think that's the Chicago dog, Spark." I broke off a piece of my hot dog and held it out for him. "Hungry?"

Spark's head appeared from Rhia's hair. Looking at me curiously, he hopped to the edge of her shoulder, sniffed my fingers, and grabbed the hot dog chunk with his little paws, eating it in two bites. It turned to ash and drifted to the ground.

Delicious, he said and launched off Rhia's shoulder, heading in the direction of Sammy's food truck.

Rhia grinned. "He's adorable, and I love him. If you ever need me to watch him, just let me know."

I laughed. "I think he does as he pleases. But yeah, he's great."

We watched Spark devour another Chicago dog that he'd likely stolen from somebody, and I felt truly happy for the first time all day.

2

Damian

I rammed my fist into the shifter's face, breaking his nose with a satisfying crunch.

His partner was already on the floor of the ring, out cold.

I ducked beneath my opponent's desperate haymaker and unleashed three fast jabs into his chest. He grunted and staggered back. I dropped my fist into his temple, and he slammed into the ropes and flopped onto the floor, barely conscious.

Finished.

I slipped out of the ring.

"Thanks," I grunted, as I tossed the shifter a fat wad of bills. It would have been one hundred thousand dollars if the duo could beat me. Instead, it was ten thousand. Unfortunately, there wasn't much point to bringing anything more than ten. The ranks of fighters were getting pretty thin.

The fights were private. That way, my opponents could claim whatever they wanted—that they'd come close to beating me, or hell, that they had. I didn't care. The truth didn't matter.

I rolled my shoulder as my healing magic began to cure my broken bones and bruises. The shifters had actually managed to land a couple of solid blows, I'd give them that. I wiped the blood off my face with a sweaty towel and headed for the dirty lockers at the back of the pit.

I'd been there too much lately, but I had a lot of shit to work through and was more than happy to stimulate the local bar economy.

I strode into the locker room, threw off my clothes, and stepped into the shower. I let the noise of the clanging pipes and steam drown out the thoughts tugging at my soul.

Or at least, I tried to.

It had been two days since I'd seen her. Two *excruciating* days since the Realm of Water. The battle with the efreet. Since banishment by the fucking *marid king*. I scrubbed my hand through my damp hair.

I hadn't had time to explain anything. Now, Matthias was out there, and Neve was in danger.

Her absence had been a shadow on my heart, as if the colors of the sky had suddenly disappeared.

From the moment I had sought a planes-walker to help me capture the djinn, I'd been able to sense Neve, tugging on my chest like an invisible cord. It was part of my FireSoul magic. Part of my curse.

I shared a fragment of an ancient dragon's soul. That covetous part of my spirit guided me toward the things that I wanted, the things that I *craved*.

When I was cast out of the Realm of Water, it was like the invisible cord had snapped. But now the feeling had returned. She was here in Magic Side. I was certain of it.

I stepped out of the dingy shower and dried off with a tattered old towel before throwing on a crisp button-down.

It was a workday, after all.

This morning, I'd sent my spies to keep an eye out for her while I worked on a plan to catch my old friend, Matthias. *The treacherous bastard.*

My cellphone buzzed, and I dug it out of my gym bag. "What?"

"Sorry to disturb you, Mr. Malek, but Miss Cross was just spotted in Exposition Park."

"Thanks." I disconnected the call.

I pulled the rest of my clothes on and headed upstairs to the public part of the pit. There weren't many people around at this time of day except a few early-morning drunks and some fighters practicing in the big ring. I shoved out of the heavy wooden door and onto the street.

Hopefully, I didn't look like hell. I hadn't looked in a mirror, and I needed to make a good impression.

Or did I? Fuck it. She'd seen all she needed to already. The façade didn't matter.

Neve would be upset, no doubt. The expressions on her face after I'd taken the efreet's magic had snapped my heart—fear, betrayal, anger. She knew for certain I was a FireSoul now, if she hadn't suspected it before.

That cursed fragment of a dragon's soul gave me the power to steal the magic of others upon their death. And I craved nothing more than power.

But I had taken the efreet's magic to protect Neve from Matthias and the djinn, monsters I had unleashed into the world. I was just leveling the playing field. I hadn't gained all of the djinn's powers—I couldn't grant wishes—but I was going to be able to burn Matthias's ambitions to the ground.

I gritted my teeth. I would have to make Neve understand that I had no choice.

Was that really true?

I crossed to where I'd parked my black Corvette, checking my watch—ten-thirty a.m.

I turned the key in the ignition, wondering why Neve hadn't gone to the Order yet. That was good for me. I couldn't risk her revealing that I was a FireSoul.

The archmages would hunt me down and either kill me or lock me up without a trial.

Fuck that.

The car rumbled to life. Releasing the clutch, I hit the gas pedal, and the car screeched away from the curb. After a couple of blocks, I turned right and headed out onto the Midway.

A few minutes later, I parked, slipped the keys into my pocket, and headed into Exposition Park. Neve was close. Her signature was like a riptide pulling me out to sea.

Ice danced up my spine, but I reigned it in. I needed to think clearly, but she was like a strong cocktail, clouding my mind.

I rounded the corner and stopped short as I caught sight of her sitting on a bench, laughing with Rhiannon. Neve's hair danced hypnotically in the wind, and her jasmine scent wrapped around me.

My chest tightened.

She was safe, for the moment. A hidden weight fell from my shoulders, and for a second, I was paralyzed, not wanting to step closer, not wanting to break her spell.

Gods, why did I feel this way? Weak. Powerless.

Steadying my breath, I started toward her. She must have felt my signature brush against her, because she turned.

Our eyes locked, and for the briefest second, I

thought I saw excitement cross her features. It was quickly replaced with anger. She jumped to her feet and took a step toward me, her eyes shooting daggers. "What are you doing here?"

Rhiannon stood beside Neve, her hand slipping to the bolas secured to her hip.

I stopped several feet short, keeping some distance between us. "Neve. We need to talk. You're not safe."

"That's *exactly* why you shouldn't be here."

I looked to Rhiannon and then to Neve. "Does she know?"

"Yes. She knows *all* of your lies," Neve shot back.

Her words stung. "Fair enough. But Matthias is still out there, and you won't be safe until we get him. You need to come with me." I stepped forward, extending my hand to her. An olive branch.

She flinched and stepped back, causing that tightness in my chest to return. "There is no *we*. And I'm not going anywhere with you."

Frustration and anger mixed with the worry I'd been carrying around for days. My voice came out rough. "You need protection, Neve. And as much as you dislike me right now, I'm the only one who can keep you safe from Matthias."

"Dislike? I *hate* you right now. You've been lying to me from the start. About what Matthias is. What you are. You've been using me." The wind began to rise around her, lifting the leaves at her feet.

I balled my fists and bit down my anger, not wanting to add fuel to the storm that was clearly rising.

Neve's eyes darkened, and the wind picked up. "If you want to do something about your *friend* Matthias, then go find out what he's up to and report it to the proper authorities!"

My blood ran hot, and something deep inside me switched on. I swore I saw flames licking down my wrists, but that must have been the sun's glare. I took a step back, willing my emotions into submission.

"Neve, this is not the place." I knew where this was going, and judging from the look on her face, it was not the time to negotiate.

Her signature overwhelmed me. Citrus. Jasmine. I could taste ozone in the air, and all of the sensations around me were magnified. The dragon inside me stirred.

Neve was far stronger now than she'd been in the desert. She had changed.

A trashcan beside the food truck blew over, sending napkins and soda cans clanking down the sidewalk. Passersby looked around, panic in their eyes.

I gritted my teeth and shoved my pride down into my chest. I wanted to rage, but this wasn't the place to work out our problems. I didn't want to draw attention to Neve. We couldn't risk revealing what she was...or, for that matter, what I was.

Her eyes blazed, and her tattoo glowed beneath her jacket.

I backed away. "For what it's worth, I'm sorry."

"Get out of here."

I turned and left, climbing into my car a minute later. Leaning back in the leather seat, I breathed in, hoping it might ease the tension that rippled through my body.

"Damnit!" I slammed my hands on the steering wheel.

This was a gods-damned mess.

Her presence—her power—made my head spin. And it was getting worse.

I gripped the wheel until my knuckles turned white. There was only one thing I could do.

I turned the ignition, and the car rumbled to life.

Find Matthias.

3

Neve

I watched Damian leave. Rage, regret, and a deep ache tormented me. Why did I feel this way?

His new aura flickered among red, green, and orange —the last stolen from the efreet. Would it dance with white light, too, one day after he stole my magic? Like in my dreams?

Rhiannon squeezed my shoulder, and I turned to her. My emotions suddenly calmed, and the wind around me abated.

"You okay?" Rhia asked.

My lip quivered, but I held back the tears. I wouldn't shed them for him. She hugged me, and I sobbed quietly into her shoulder.

Once I'd gotten it out, I stood up and stiffened my back. "Now that that's done, let's find Gretchen."

We headed down a path leading toward the Hall of Inquiry.

Rhia glanced around. "Where's Spark?"

I hadn't seen him since Damian showed up. "Not sure. Like I said, he's got a mind of his own."

I turned back toward Sammy's food truck, but Spark was gone.

We walked in silence, but my mind churned over the words I'd exchanged with Damian. Had I really said I hated him? I winced.

I *should* hate him. But I didn't. I couldn't explain my feelings, and that infuriated me.

"Detective Holloway!" a man shouted from across the square in front of the Hall.

"Oh, fates." Rhiannon's cheeks flushed, and she tilted her head down. "Keep walking."

I scanned the square, searching for the cause of Rhia's sudden nerves. "Whoa." The word escaped my mouth as I spotted him. Tall, dark hair, olive skin. I glanced at Rhia with a smirk. "Who's *that*?"

She grabbed my arm and hurried me up the steps to the Hall. "Nobody."

I glanced back at the guy, who was suddenly looking confused. "He doesn't look like a nobody. In fact, he looks like a hottie. Shifter?"

Rhiannon shot me a devilish grin and peeked over

her shoulder at him. "Could you sense him? But no, he's not a thing, and we're not talking about him."

I smiled. Rhiannon didn't keep guys around long. She also didn't like to kiss and tell—though she'd always interrogated me mercilessly about anyone I met.

We walked through the Hall of Inquiry's front doors, drawing stares from the people in the foyer. "Why is everybody staring at us, Rhia?" I murmured.

"They're not staring at *us*. They're staring at *you*." She nodded at Detective Harlow as she towed me to the elevator. Harlow was one of the nice ones.

Shit. Everybody knew that I was responsible for the efreet's attack. They must have, given the icicles they'd shot at me. *Just* what I needed as a newbie detective.

"Don't worry, they're only surprised that you're alive. Everybody assumed you were dead when we saw the wreckage," Rhia said, tapping the button for the fourth floor.

A punch to my gut. I hadn't realized how worried Rhia must have been. "Sorry," I said as the elevator doors shut, and we shot up.

Seconds later, the doors opened to a room filled with detectives and researchers making phone calls and shuffling papers.

I caught sight of Lieutenant Gretchen in her office. The walls were glass, and she was leaning over her desk, shouting something into the phone. She looked up as

Rhiannon and I stepped into the room...and so did everybody else.

Gretchen strode out of her office, the lines on her face more visible than normal. "Detective Cross. Glad to have you back. In my office, *now.*"

I looked at Rhiannon. "Well, that was quick."

She squeezed my arm, and we weaved through the morass of blank stares.

Rhiannon shut the door to the L.T.'s office, and I sat in one of the low, plastic chairs in front of Gretchen's desk—the most uncomfortable chairs ever made.

Gretchen stood behind her desk. "Where in the names of the gods have you been, Nevaeh? Do you know what we've been doing, trying to find you?"

I placed my hands in my lap. "Sorry, Lieutenant. I would have called, but I was in the Realm of Water, and there's limited cell reception there."

Where the heck was this cockiness coming from?

Gretchen's face turned red, and she rested her palms on the desk, eyes boring into mine.

"What Neveah meant to say," Rhiannon said, taking a seat on the chair next to mine, "is that she heroically drew the efreet, who was wreaking havoc on Old Mud City, into the Realm of Water. Where she killed it."

Gretchen's eyes widened at those final words. She looked between Rhia and me. "You're serious?"

"Yes, L.T. I killed the flaming bastard."

And I had help from a FireSoul, by the way. Minor detail.

Gretchen collapsed into her chair with a sigh. "Heavens, Neve. How do you keep getting yourself into these situations?"

Well, let's see. *It all started when I agreed to work with one of the most notorious crime lords in Magic Side—Damian Malek.* Fat chance I could tell her that.

"You're telling me," I said, feigning ignorance.

Gretchen pulled out a notebook and pen. "All right. Start from the beginning."

I told her everything. Well, everything minus working with Damian and him being a FireSoul, Amal helping sneak us into Helwan, and me being a half-djinn. So basically, I didn't tell her much at all. The Order had a habit of locking up people who couldn't control their magic—*like me*—in Bentham, Magic Side's high-security prison.

Gretchen leaned back in her chair, clicking her pen. "If I didn't know you better, I'd say you were full of shit. But you're one of my top people, and it's too bizarre to not be true."

Well, that was something. My story sounded wild to my ears when I heard it out loud. Any other lieutenant would have fired me and locked me up. I was glad I'd stopped putting salt in Gretchen's coffee.

Technically, I hadn't been in the office long enough to do so, but that was neither here nor there.

I stood, stretching my legs, and walked over to the water jug in the corner. My mouth was bone-dry after the epic I'd just told twice. But as I filled my cup, a low rumble vibrated the floor, faint at first before growing.

What the...?

I looked at Rhiannon and Gretchen, who seemed to be wondering the same thing, and the room suddenly rocked violently. My water spilled as I lost my balance and crashed into the wall.

"What the hell was that?" Rhiannon asked.

The shaking stopped.

I glanced down at Rhia's jacket, which I'd just soaked with water. "It felt like an earthquake."

Gretchen looked at me with a flat expression on her face. "We're in Chicago."

Fair point. Tornadoes, *maybe*.

The rumbling resumed, and I braced myself as the building shook again, dislodging the fluorescent light above Gretchen's desk.

"Shit!" She wheeled her chair back as one side of the light dropped and dangled from the ceiling.

The tremors stopped.

"You're right. This is no earthquake." Closing my eyes, I focused on the slight vibrations that still reverberated through the walls in what felt like bursts. They seemed to be coming from the lower levels of the building.

Adrenaline suddenly surged through me. "The Archives!"

The Hall's Archives were located in an underground

chamber that sunk sixty-seven floors below Lake Michigan—stupid design, if you asked me. I raced out of the room, heading for the stairwell.

Rhiannon caught up as I skidded around a corner, nearly colliding with a troll from registration. The troll grunted at me, but fear had taken over, and there was no time for niceties.

"What is it?" Rhia asked, as we sprinted down the stairwell and burst through the door leading to the second-floor skybridge.

"I think the Archives are under attack." I slowed as we neared the magical doors to the Archives' upper gallery. The scenes that normally danced across them flickered and flashed like they'd gone haywire.

A cold rush of air blasted into us as I wrenched open the doors, followed by a thunderous noise echoing from deep below. My heart sank. "Oh, no."

I ran to the balcony that overlooked the bookstacks and peered into the circular chamber. An icy updraft hit me.

Imps darted through the air, clutching books to their chests, and a bubbling noise rose from the darkness below.

"Run!" An imp rushed past me, fleeing through the open door. "The chamber is flooding! Get out now!"

A burning rage rushed over me. "We have to stop this."

"What can we do?" Rhia asked, determination in her voice.

The outer walls of the Archive must have been breached. An attack. An attack by someone powerful with unlimited resources.

Matthias.

"You find the archmages. I'm going down there," I said, kicking off the slippers Amira had given me.

I handed Rhia my phone, and she frowned. "What? You're actually serious?"

"Yes. I'm going to hold back the water, but I'll need some help. Find Archmage DeLoren. Tell him I need a powerful spell. Tell him that Matthias and his genies are here."

I climbed onto the balcony railing, and Rhiannon nodded. "Be careful!"

The lights that lined the lower recesses of the chamber had gone out, and those on the upper levels flickered. I stared into the darkness below, and fear clawed at my nerves.

I freaking *hated* dark water. But this was my temple, and it was under attack.

Taking an unsteady breath, I dove off the ledge.

4

Damian

Frustration tore at me as I pulled up in front of Matthias's house. What was left of it, at least, a burned-out shell surrounded by withered and blackened flowers.

Matthias was gone. His notes, gone. Any evidence, gone.

Yellow police tape cordoned off the area. This wasn't an accident—it was arson. Matthias had destroyed everything.

I'd had my people scour the place already, so I knew what to expect. Still, I wanted to see it for myself.

I slammed the car door shut, ducked under the police tape, and pushed my way through the twisted iron gate. Somehow, the burned wreckage called to me and my new fire powers. The efreet's magic surged in my veins, burning to be released.

Guilt tugged at me. I had sworn not to take powers, not to feed the dragon within—the part of me that was a FireSoul. But I had also sworn to protect Neve.

We had killed the efreet. And I had made my choice. I'd ripped the magic from his soul, his command over fire, even his ability to planes-walk.

I was no efreet, though. I couldn't grant wishes. That was a different kind of magic, one that couldn't be stolen. One that was a deep part of your being.

I kicked a blackened beam over, trying to clear away the debris in what had once been Matthias's office.

Ashes.

I need to stop Matthias before he brings heaven down on us all.

So where was he?

The searing citadel. I would start there.

Closing my eyes, I concentrated on the citadel and the place I'd come to know all too well—the dungeon.

I had planes-walked many times now with Neve. I knew what it entailed.

I focused my magic and erupted through the ether. The cosmos tore at me, g-forces threatening to rip me apart, jerking me in every direction before sucking me through a wormhole between worlds.

Pain arced through me as I spiraled through the sky,

barely able to focus on my destination. Then my feet slammed into stone.

Everything was dark. Summoning a ball of fire to my left hand, I scanned the empty space. Not a sign of life.

I drew my smoking blade from the ether, coated it with fire, and headed through the dungeon's gate. Shadows shifted along the walls. The silence of the deserted place was haunting.

I found the armory, but it was looted and abandoned. Then the kitchens. No sign of life. I searched the citadel, calling Matthias's name, dragging my flaming blade along the obsidian walls, but there was no response.

Irritation gnawed at me, and I glanced through a window at the boiling lava lake in the caldera. Was the tower listing? The horizon seemed wrong.

I saw no guards on the parapets or on the grounds at the base of the tower. The citadel had been utterly abandoned.

I cursed, my blade burning for a fight.

Just days ago, Matthias and the efreet had been amassing an army. Had they deserted the cause?

Unlikely.

The citadel suddenly shuddered as if in answer to my thought. Without the efreet's magic, the fortress was slowly sinking into the volcano. The same had happened to the djinn's palace in the Realm of Air after we'd trapped him—it crumbled to dust and ashes.

Good reason to pack up shop. So where had the army gone?

I pushed deeper into the citadel.

After countless hallways, I entered a massive chamber supported by tall, thin pillars, one I hadn't seen before. The flame from my blade danced up the walls, but darkness shrouded the ceiling above. A massive ring of runes filled the space, thirty feet in diameter, at least. A teleportation portal.

I didn't recognize the runes, but maybe Neve or someone in Magic Side could. I pulled out my cellphone and snapped several photos.

What else was here?

The citadel suddenly quaked, more violently this time. Vibrations surged through the walls, turning stone into waves. I dropped to the floor as a tsunami of magic overwhelmed me, tearing at the corners of my sanity and dissolving me into the ether.

I was planes-walking, but not of my own accord.

I strained against the magic, but the cosmos prevailed. A thunderclap jolted through my body, and then everything went quiet.

I was still in the citadel. The scent of sulfur and acid hung in the air.

What the hell just happened?

Surging to my feet, I pushed through the citadel, my flaming blade drawn to light the way. The corridors of the fortress were still deserted as I climbed a stairwell, and then I pushed my way through an iron door and out onto one of the tower's balconies.

Cold air cut my skin and burned my lungs as I gazed into the purple sky.

The citadel was no longer in the Realm of Fire. Matthias and his genies must have teleported it somewhere else.

"Clever bastard."

5

Neve

The icy updraft buffeted my body as I launched off the railing into the pit of the Archives. The sound of rushing water echoed through the chamber, growing louder as I descended, drowning out my pounding heartbeat.

A bright light appeared to my left, and I glanced sideways. "Spark!"

I'm here. The little dragon's wings hugged his body as he dove beside me. A wave of relief washed over me.

As we plummeted, books lining the upper shelves of the chamber whizzed by in the flickering light. At least three quarters of the shelves were still dry. If I could just stop the—

"Watch out!" screamed an imp.

Spark dodged him, and I narrowly avoided a collision with two other imps who flew out of the dark recesses of the chamber, clutching books to their chests.

With a burst of wind, I slowed my descent into the darkness. The last thing I needed was to clip an imp on my way down.

Hovering at my side, Spark began to glow brighter than I'd ever seen him, casting light on the shadows below.

I cursed under my breath as I took in the damage. The lower levels of the Archives were flooded. The lake water that helped stabilize the temperature of the Archives during the summer now threatened to destroy the entire collection. Books bobbed and churned on the surface of the rapidly rising water. At the rate it was going, the Archives would be completely inundated in a matter of minutes.

I can't follow you down there, Spark said.

Of course. Fire and water. Opposites. *That* was why Spark hadn't followed us to the Realm of Water during our battle with the efreet.

"Okay. Stay here and shine the light on me so I can see."

Be careful! Something's down there, I can sense it.

Dread seeped into my soul, but there was no time. The water was rising quickly. With not a second to spare, I dove into the turbid water. Icy daggers shot through my chest, and I fought the urge to gasp. I created an air bubble around my face and jetted down-ward on a stream of air, the bubble acting like a mask, allowing me to breathe and see.

The pounding of my heart returned in the silence of the water. I could have used Amira—a marid—as backup right about now.

Books and shelving floated aimlessly in the water, and I used my arm to shield my head from the debris as I dove deeper. A piece of wood sliced my forearm, but the cold water dulled the pain.

The bottom of the chamber finally appeared thirty feet below, littered with chunks of concrete and lime-stone. One of them was larger than the others, but I couldn't discern it in the faint glow of Spark's light filtering down from above.

These walls were at least ten feet thick, so whatever had removed those chunks was powerful. Dynamite, maybe?

I strained against the surge of water pushing me upward and scanned the space for signs of where the water was seeping in.

Goosebumps shot across my skin, and I froze.

Had that piece of concrete just moved?

I blinked twice, trying to focus on the shapes that littered the floor. Then the largest one of them shifted before darting across the bottom into shadow.

Shit.

I floated in the freezing water, waiting for the

monster to attack. The only thing worse than dark water was unknown things *in* the water.

My body jerked as an explosive sound ricocheted through the chamber, followed by two more. A cloud of debris rose from where the thing had disappeared. Was it tearing apart the building? The surge of water increased, forcing me upward.

It was now or never.

I swam down into the shadowy depths of the Archives, looking around wildly for the monster. But I found nothing but concrete debris. Had it been a trick of the eye?

Despite being numb, my skin tingled. I grasped a boulder to keep from being pushed back by the inflow of water and inspected the walls.

Half a dozen giant cracks wound around the chamber, like something heavy had crashed into them. *From the inside.* Nothing about the damage looked like an explosive device.

A chill snaked up my spine as the tingling sensation began to burn. Was that a magic signature? The more I focused on it, the more I sensed it—rotten and acidic, like battery acid. It filled the space.

Heart pounding, I slowly glanced over my shoulder. An inky shape slithered behind a boulder, and I spun and unleashed a burst of air in its direction, tempering it so as not to damage the cracked wall behind.

Bubbles clouded my vision, then dissipated.

And then the creature appeared, moving like mercury and growing. Its magic unleashed a wave of nausea over me. As the monster flashed by, something sharp raked my thigh, like a thousand burning knives slicing my flesh. I screamed as an explosive force slammed me backward into the wall, knocking the air from my lungs.

Thank goodness for the air bubble around my face. I would have drowned.

Ears ringing and lungs heaving, I squinted through the red-tinted water at the gaping hole in the wall in front of me.

It measured five feet in diameter, *at least*.

Had the thing swum through?

Wincing at the pain in my back and thigh, I pushed off and jetted to a boulder below the hole, where I braced myself between it and the wall. The powerful surge of water pushed down on me with a crushing force.

My heartbeat pounded in my chest, reminding me how *not* okay I was with this. But what choice did I have?

My palms stung as magic pooled in my hands. I wasn't exactly sure what I planned to do, or if it would work. But I had to try something, and I wanted to close this gaping hole before that thing came back.

Please, fates, let luck be on my side today.

I unleashed a wall of air at the hole, hoping it might create a seal. Instead, it pushed through and dissipated.

Apparently, luck *wasn't* on my side at the moment.

I tried again, this time directing several slow but steady streams of air along the sides of the hole. The air pocket stuck to the concrete and slowly spread, pooling together and creating a seal over the opening. The inflow of water stopped, but I could feel it pushing hard against my magical barrier.

"Bingo," I murmured.

Suddenly, the seal burst, and a rush of water returned. The surge pushed me into the back wall of the chamber, and a dull pain shot through my left shoulder blade.

Third time was the charm, right?

Using the wall at my back to brace myself, I repeated the process, creating a pocket of air over the gaping hole. This time, I didn't let up, but kept unleashing a steady stream of air at the seal...and it worked. The water stopped flowing in.

As long as my magic held, so would the seal.

Now what?

The chattering of my teeth replaced the ringing in my ears. How long could I stay down here? My arms trembled, and it was difficult to keep them up. I closed my eyes, willing my mind to warm me. My arms were so numb, I almost didn't notice the hand on my shoulder until it squeezed.

I jumped, eyes bolting open.

A man I didn't recognize stared back at me, illuminated by a glowing orb strapped to his belt. Bubbles streamed from the strange full-face mask he wore. It wasn't connected to a scuba tank or a hose, so it must have been magical.

He turned and kicked over to the air bubble. His tan trousers and blue T-shirt floated around him as he inspected the damaged wall. This guy definitely wasn't Archmage DeLoren. Turning back to me, he made the okay sign with his thumb and index finger.

Okay? There was nothing *okay* about any of this. My body had morphed into a convulsing popsicle, my thigh was ripped open, and it was taking every ounce of energy to stay focused.

The guy swam to the middle of the chamber, pulled off his fins, and planted his feet on the floor.

I watched him, my brain too taxed to guess what he was up to.

He closed his eyes, and his lips began moving. A soft glow emanated from his chest, and then from the backs of his hands, which floated by his side.

I waited for something to happen, but nothing did. Just the glowing.

DeLoren sent a rookie.

Panic fluttered in my chest. I couldn't feel my arms anymore. I couldn't feel anything but the slight current that began pushing down on me.

I looked up and blinked. The books and flotsam that had been drifting overhead suddenly froze in place.

The glowing from Rookie's chest began to increase, and so did the current. It was almost as if the water in the chamber were being sucked down, yet everything floating in the water remained still.

Hypothermia, or blood loss, had *clearly* made me delusional.

I shook my head and kept pouring my magic into the seal on the hole, because I was pretty certain it was still the *only* thing preventing all of Lake Michigan from pouring in at this moment.

My gaze fell to the seal, and I did a double-take. Flashes of light streaked across the wall of air covering the hole. I looked up. The water level in the chamber was dropping.

Holy fates. Rookie *did* know what he was doing.

Excitement surged through me, and I forced my arms to stay upright as I pushed more magic into the seal, making sure it wouldn't collapse.

A minute later, our heads broke the surface, and Spark appeared. He flapped around my head, looking agitated. *Neve! You're as pale as coconut gelato. What can I do?*

I released the pocket of air around my face and looked at Rookie. His mask was still on, and he appeared deeply focused on reciting whatever spell was drawing out the water.

"Co-old," I said through chattering teeth, noticing

that all of the floating books and debris were gone. What the...?

I will help, Spark said.

With every second that passed, the water dropped inches, and soon, it lapped at my waist.

Spark shifted into a ball of light and drifted through me, disappearing when he hit my chest. Warmth cascaded through me, spreading to my legs and arms and fingers.

In a matter of minutes, Rookie had drained all but a shallow puddle on the floor. I still had no idea where all of the flotsam had gone. He'd better not have sucked my precious books out with the water.

Rookie ripped off his mask and looked at me, worry crossing his face as his gaze dropped to my wounded thigh. "I need you to hold on for just a few more minutes."

An Australian?

Still channeling my magic and too exhausted to speak, I nodded. He turned and strode to the gaping hole in the chamber, placing his hands on the seal I'd created. The light from his hands flared, and I turned my face, shielding my eyes from the onslaught. I watched Rookie's shadow on the back wall where I stood, his hands moving up and down. Then they stopped, and the blinding light subsided.

I glanced up and met Rookie's gaze. Over his shoulder, the gaping hole and all of the cracks were covered with some sort of crystalline stone.

Problem solved.

I released my magic and collapsed.

Rookie caught me before I landed on my face. He lowered me to the ground, cradling my back in his arms.

Consciousness flickered in and out, and I relaxed when warmth wrapped around me, easing the shivers that convulsed my body.

My eyes fluttered open. Rookie stared down at me, his sandy blond hair still damp, framing a perfectly cut jaw and a pair of topaz eyes. His magic signature poured over me—the feel of windswept plains, the sound of thundering hooves, rich aromas of hickory and earth.

"Welcome back," he said with that slight Australian accent.

I sat up and winced at the bright light that exited my chest—Spark. He shifted back into his dragon form and hovered beside Rookie and me. *Better now?*

"Yes. Thanks, Spark."

I wasn't sure how Spark did that trick, but it had saved me on the airship and again today. I was grateful. Though I'd have to figure out some way for him to swim...

"Your companion?" Rookie asked, inspecting my wounded thigh.

"He's a fire sprite named Spark. Spark, meet Roo—" I paused and pretended to cough. "What's your name?"

"Ethan. Do you mind if I fix this?" He gestured to the three gashes that peeked out of my ripped jeans, oozing blood. It looked worse than I'd thought.

"Sure." I stared at him suspiciously. Healing magic was an extremely rare gift.

I flinched as he placed a hand beside the wound— not out of pain, but because of the tingling warmth that cascaded through me. He raised his eyes to mine, and I looked away, feeling heat rush to my cheeks.

I wasn't attracted to him—not to say he wasn't gorgeous—but the intimacy of healing magic was something I'd only shared with one other person.

Damian.

My chest tightened.

"You were great back there. I've never seen anyone use magic like that. What are you?"

Panic flared as I searched for words but came up short.

Ethan's magic suddenly released, and I looked down at my thigh, thankful for the distraction. The torn flesh of the wound under my ripped jeans was smooth and pink, as if I'd just stepped out of a hot shower.

"You like to keep your cards close to the vest. I understand." He stood and extended his hand to me, his lips curling into a smile. "Will you at least tell me your name?"

I took his hand, and he pulled me to my feet. "Neve. Thanks for everything...I—"

"Neve! Are you down there?" Rhiannon's voice echoed faintly from sixty-seven floors above.

"Yes. We're okay. Be right up!" I shouted back to her. I stepped toward Ethan. "Hold on to me, and I'll fly us out of here."

Ethan shot me a wry grin, then stepped close and placed his hands on my hips.

I slung my arms around his torso. "You're going to have to do better than that if you expect me to carry you."

He cleared his throat and wrapped his arms around me.

I lifted us up on a steady gust of wind. The bookshelves lining the chamber flew by, and I wondered again where in gods' names all of those floating books and debris went.

I slowed our ascent as we neared the upper balcony, then landed beside Rhiannon, who was looking rather ashen. "Thank gods, you're okay," she said, but did a double-take when she saw Ethan. "Where's Archmage DeLoren?"

Good question.

If DeLoren had sent Ethan in his place, this guy must be pretty powerful, and judging from what I'd seen him do down there, he was.

Ethan bent down and tied the laces of the shoes he'd apparently shrugged off before jumping into the pit. "He got called to Bentham with the others."

"Bentham? Why would he go there?" I asked as Rhia handed me my phone.

She looked at me, worry in her eyes. "Probably because it was attacked shortly after you dove into the chamber."

Bentham—home to some of Magica's worst criminals—was under attack. The words sunk into my brain, and I knew the timing of these two incidents was no mere coincidence.

This was coordinated, and the Archives was a distraction.

Double shit.

6

Neve

I slipped out the back of the Hall of Inquiry and leapt into the air. Flying in daylight was risky, but I had to get to Bentham Prison. This attack had to be Matthias's doing. Only the fates knew what he was up to.

Something terrible, I was certain.

I flew over rooftops, staying low and out of sight, avoiding the powerlines. Clotheslining myself was not how I wanted it all to end.

I dumped my depleted magic into the flight, urging myself to go faster. The rows of brick buildings gave way to Shoreline Park, and in seconds, I was soaring out over Lake Michigan, shielded from view by the spell that concealed Magic Side.

I sped toward Bentham Island, which sat squarely in the channel between Magic Side and Chicago, isolated in the icy water like Alcaraz. Two imposing perimeter walls and a smaller magical dome that prevented teleportation and flight made it one of the most secure locations in Magic Side. The defense meant I'd have to go in the front gate, but I definitely didn't want anyone to see me flying up to the door. I would tell the Order what I was at some point. Not now.

Hopefully, I could land out of sight on the shore and make my way around. I didn't know the lay of the land, but I'd figure it out, come hell or high water.

I dropped low to the lake to conceal my approach. Water sprayed up as I rocketed over the waves, chilling my skin.

Apart from the prison, the island was a desolate crag. The looming walls reached the water's edge in many places, leaving me little room to make a landing. Worse, sleepless gargoyles along the parapets monitored the grounds and made sure no one approached unchallenged.

That was going to be a problem.

If they saw me flying straight at the prison, they might attack and ask questions later. If they were otherwise occupied, it would mean Matthias was here, and I didn't want him spotting me, either.

I called my magic and shot a sheet of wind at the

lake ahead of me. Water sprayed into the air, and I wove it into a dense fog to conceal my approach.

Suspicious, *yeah*, but hopefully, it would serve my purpose.

The sound of the waves breaking against the shore intensified, and I slowed my approach. Boulders rose out of the mist around me, and soon, I was below the perimeter wall of the prison. The base extended deep into the water here, so it would be impossible to walk around.

I drifted through the fog. Fragments of stone and mortar were strewn around the base of the walls, and my heart sank. Someone, or something, had done some serious damage.

I skirted the perimeter until I reached a large concrete platform, probably the primary dock. I blew a gust of wind to thin the fog, peeked out, and spotted no one. With that, I flew forward and gently alighted.

"Neve?"

I gasped, and my heart stopped. It only started beating again once I recognized the voice. "Holy smokes, L.T., you nearly killed me."

She was standing just inside the gateway of the prison—well, in what was left of the gateway. The entire thing had been reduced to rubble. Worse, there were bluecoats milling around inside, taking pictures, documenting the damage. That meant whatever had attacked the prison was long gone.

I was too late.

I picked my way through the scattered debris. "Godzilla attack?"

Gretchen put away her tablet and ignored my question. "You can fly."

It wasn't a question.

I gave a halfhearted grin and shrugged. "Yes?"

She nodded and looked out at the conspicuous patch of mist I'd dragged along with me. "Useful. And I'm guessing you can make fog now?"

"I guess."

"Right. Well, make sure you file the appropriate paperwork for acquired powers."

"I'm not sure I want anyone to know, L.T."

She glowered. "Not optional. File the paperwork by *Thursday*. It's my ass and yours if someone finds out and you haven't disclosed."

I swallowed. Well, the cat was going to get out of the bag. Hopefully, not *all* of the cats, because I had a lot of cats. I could disclose the flying, but not the whole becoming a hurricane, destroying a neighborhood, and maybe possibly being able to grant wishes thing.

She took my measure. "You look...disheveled. And wet."

I stood a little straighter and spoke directly. "I had to save the Archives. They flooded. Went for a swim and got them sealed up with a little help from Ethan. Also got a touch of hypothermia, but I shook it off. Flew right here."

"Well done," she said, and looked back down at her tablet. "Glad the archmage was there to help."

"Archmage?"

"Ethan."

Whoops. Now who seemed like a rookie?

I swallowed hard. I needed to recover because this conversation was going a little pear-shaped. I used my best I'm-a-detective-now voice and tossed my hair. "So what's the situation here, L.T? I'm here to help."

The display would have come off better if Gretchen wasn't already walking away.

I hurried after her, passing through the shattered gateway into a field of destruction. Rubble and clods of turf littered the compound. The second wall had been breached, too, and the grounds were a quagmire of residual ponds.

"The situation here is wet, Neve. Very wet." She nodded to the bluecoats wading around the puddles. "It seems to have been a very controlled tsunami."

"The marid?"

I was referring the genie Damian and I had found in Helwan. The one Matthias had stolen from us and now had under his control.

"Probably." She cocked her chin up, and I followed her gaze.

Gargoyles stared down impassively from the parapets, assessing the activity below. Above them, the dome—

The dome was corrupted. Veins of shadow slithered across its surface, slowly spreading like roots. They seemed to be drawing their power from a series of strange inscriptions arranged across the structure. I sensed it now that I had time to focus—dark, corrosive magic that reeked of rotting fish and sounded like nails on a chalkboard. I had been too preoccupied with my arrival before to notice.

This was bad.

"What *is* that?" I asked.

"We don't know. Some kind of spell. Our seer is struggling to decode it." Gretchen cocked an eyebrow at me. "Any chance you know? You're wrapped up in all of this, it seems."

I swallowed hard. True. "I have no idea, but I might know someone who does."

"Get on it. We need all the eyes we can get."

I nodded and grabbed my phone, then made a quick call to Lily DuVoir, the curse diviner. She almost never left the Dockside Dens, but I hoped—fingers crossed— that she might assist even though she generally worked for the criminal Underworld. She had helped me out in a few tough spots before.

The call rang through, and a woman with an alluring French accent answered. "Hello?"

"Madame DuVoir? I need a big favor."

After explaining the situation, I muted my phone and turned to Gretchen. "She doesn't like going out, but she'll do it. Though we'll owe a favor to the Dockside boss."

Gretchen nodded. "Fine. Do it."

"Thanks, Lily. It's a deal." I hung up.

Everything in Magic Side—the whole magical world, really—ran on friend networks and favors. With there being so few Magica, and everyone having unique talents, favors were the only hard currency. Even the police and crime lords exchanged favors—like now. It kept things fluid. Running. Everyone could make something out of what gifts they had.

I surveyed the scene.

Not good at all.

The prison looked intact, though it appeared to be infected with dark magic as well.

The central prison building was a ring-shaped fortress called the Panopticon. Its design made it possible for a handful of guards in the center to watch all of the inmates at once without the inmates knowing whether they were under surveillance.

The design dated back to the eighteenth century, though Bentham wasn't built until the 1920s. It was a bit out of date now with CCTV, but the Order loved things that sent the message, *We are watching you.* While old-timers still called it the Panopticon, the rest of us—

guards, cops, and criminals—called it "the ol' stone donut."

I nodded to the Panopticon. "Is the donut okay?"

"Some structural damage. It's been infected with the same dark magic," Gretchen said.

Two sorcerers were using telekinesis to raise chunks of broken stone, position them in the walls, and melt them in place.

Gretchen followed my eyes. "They should have this rebuilt soon, at least to a serviceable level. Obviously, it will need some new enchantments."

My heart pounded out a worried rhythm. Something didn't add up. We could rebuild the walls quickly, so what was the purpose of this attack?

I bit my lip. "Do you think Matthias or the genies will strike somewhere else?"

Gretchen shrugged. "At the moment, you're the expert on him, so you tell me. I'm not even sure what the objective here was. The Panopticon is intact. The dome isn't even down. Maybe we'll understand more once the curse diviner gets here."

"The attack on the Archives was a diversion, pulling away resources from here. I'm worried that this is a diversion, too."

"Could be."

With *that* troubling thought in mind, I helped to secure the perimeter and document damage while we waited for Madame DuVoir. The dark magic infecting the dome was growing stronger, assaulting all of my senses now.

Relief flooded through me when forty minutes later, the deep rumble of an engine drew me to the concrete dock outside the gate. A heavily armed gunboat full of shifters and marsh men pulled up.

Gretchen came to my side.

"Geez," I said. "These guys don't mess around."

She shrugged. "They like to show off their toys. But they know they can't get away with using them."

One of the marsh men helped a woman wearing a dark cowl out of the boat. She glided across the stone, stopped short of us, and turned her head. "Neve. Good to see you again so soon after your last visit."

Gretchen raised an eyebrow, and I blanched. I really didn't want my last visit to the Dockside to come up at the moment. I had helped the Devil of Darkvale—the vampire crime lord that ran Guild City—sneak into the Archives. That was a fireable offense. Then I sneaked him into the Dockside Dens to see Lily, irritating the Dockside boss.

Favors. Everything was favors.

Unfortunately, the favors for the Devil had caused Lily some unnecessary complications, and she was giving me a gentle reminder. On the other hand, she made fifty thousand pounds on the deal, so I wasn't too worried about her end of the bargain.

I pushed ahead. "Gretchen, this is Madame DuVoir, the curse diviner. An old friend."

Gretchen extended her hand. "Madame DuVoir, thank you for coming on such short notice."

Lily tipped her head slightly. "I am glad to be of service. The Dockside boss is also glad to be of service. What can I do?"

We brought her to the perimeter of the anti-teleportation dome. The twisting veins of dark magic infecting the dome made my stomach turn.

She stepped off the walkway into the churned earth so she could get close to the dome and the inscriptions that gave it power. She sniffed. "Is this the only thing that is infected?"

"The Panopticon, too," Gretchen said.

"Hm. Let me look at it."

We headed into the compound, navigating our way around pools of water and mounds of rock and torn-up turf. The tsunami had punched through both perimeter walls and piled rubble along the base of the Panopticon itself. Some of the outbuildings were completely demolished.

I sighed with relief. No bodies.

Gretchen cursed as her boot sunk deep in the ground, muddy water pouring in over the top.

I grabbed her hand and pulled her up, and she nodded to my feet, which were floating a quarter inch off the ground. "Must be nice to fly."

Dang. I'd hoped no one would notice. I let my shoes sink slightly into the mud so that it looked a little more realistic, then gave Gretchen a boost with a little gust of wind and winked. "Ever wish you were born a werebat?"

Gretchen narrowed her eyes. "No."

I was *real* quiet the rest of the way.

The curved walls of the donut had narrow, barred windows. I could see there was extensive structural damage as we approached. Cracks in the stone were filled with sinister dark magic, flowing and working away at both the walls and the enchantments that protected them.

"This is bad." Lily flipped back her hood, revealing a youthful face with dark, curly hair and bright eyes. The bangles around her wrists jangled as she reached out toward the walls.

I started forward. "Lily, careful. That's some seriously dark magic."

She winked. "Don't worry, love. I know dark magic. It doesn't bother with me."

She clutched her amber necklace and began chanting, and the veins of darkness wormed their way toward her. She reached out and grabbed one, twining it around her fingers and speaking softly to it, almost cooing. Her gentle movements and beauty were mesmerizing.

Lily turned back to us, her eyes completely black.

"These are devouring curses. It is not one, but many. They are very strong and multiplying."

"Multiplying?" I cocked an eyebrow.

"They are like sea worms devouring the hull of a ship. They will eat away the enchantments and multiply. Soon, they will consume all of the magic. The protective dome will fall. The wards on the Panopticon will fall. The anti-magic field inside will fall. The curses will consume it all."

And of course, release hundreds of highly dangerous criminals into the world.

My stomach reeled as panic flooded my veins.

Gretchen met Lily's eyes with a cold stare. "How long?"

"Roughly three days, maybe less."

"Can you break the curse?"

Lily shook her head and raised her cowl. "I could get rid of some of them. But there are too many now, and they are multiplying."

Great. Prolific curse worms.

Gretchen frowned. "Can we cast new wards?"

"The curse will eat those spells, too. Become stronger. Multiply faster. It is a virus. I'm sorry."

Shit.

"Is there anything we can do?" I asked.

"Yes." She closed her eyes, then opened them again. They were like the sea now, limitless and blue. "This curse was cast by a powerful marid, a water genie. To break the spell, you must kill it or banish it from this plane. Then the magic will weaken and fade."

Despair cut through me. I met Gretchen's eyes and shook my head.

We had gotten lucky killing the efreet. We'd pulled him into the Realm of Water, where he was weak. That trick probably wouldn't work again. Worse, he had nearly killed us on his own. Matthias, the marid, and the djinn would be impossible to take down, and it was unlikely that they would let the same thing happen again.

I clenched my teeth. "And if we can't?"

Lily shrugged. "Then you better find a way to contain several hundred extremely powerful, blood-thirsty supernaturals."

7

Damian

The ether deposited me in front of Matthias's house, where I'd planes-walked to the Searing Citadel earlier. Smoke wafted from my clothes, and my lungs burned.

Fuck. It was worse than I'd thought.

My phone buzzed once, then twice as I crossed the scorched lawn to my car. It always took a minute to get reception after planes-walking.

I reached into my pocket for my keys and pulled out the phone as it launched into a vibrating fit. Unless there was an emergency or a new bounty posted, my phone never went off like this.

I glanced at the stream of messages that flashed across the screen and tensed.

Attack on Bentham Prison. Bounties expected on escaped criminals.

Order's Archives have been hit. Casualties unknown.

Worry streaked through me as I jumped in the driver's seat and cranked the ignition. Neve worked in the Archives. Hell, she'd probably returned there after I'd confronted her in the park.

I hit the gas and sped toward the Hall of Inquiry. The buzzing from my phone didn't let up as new messages flooded in from the Network, the criminal Underworld's messaging system.

I cursed as the phone rang, Jacob's name appearing on the screen.

Jacob was my right-hand operative. He monitored the Underworld's back channels, relaying information to me and my operatives on threats and bounties, and any useful data that passed through the Network.

"What's going on?" I asked, weaving around a Honda SUV.

"The Order's Archives are flooded, and the Hall is under lockdown. Bentham was hit by a rogue tsunami an hour ago. Damage seems minimal, but the dome might be failing. Order cops have reached out to the Dockside Dens for assistance."

The Dockside Dens? That was a surprise. What in the hell was going on?

"What's the status on the Archives?"

"No word yet. Also, nobody has stepped forward

claiming credit. Might be Les Libérés, judging from the coordinated attack."

Les Libérés—the Freed—was an extremist group of ex-criminals whose primary aim was to undermine Order authority.

"No." I clutched the steering wheel, tires screeching as I pulled onto 56th Street street. "This was Matthias. Keep me updated, Jacob."

I hung up and parked the car along Exposition Park, a block from the Hall of Inquiry. Order guards in blue uniforms streamed out the front doors, some taking up position on the stairs, while others disappeared around back. Securing the perimeter, no doubt. They wouldn't stand a chance against Matthias and his genies. Or Bentham's convicts, if they escaped.

The exterior of the building was shielded in an anti-magic aura. That was something, at least.

I got out of the car and dialed Neve. She'd lost her phone in Helwan, but she'd likely have picked up a replacement. The line rang five times but went to voicemail.

There was no other choice. I was going in.

Sirens wailed in the distance as I headed down the tree-lined walkway, Magic Side's disaster warning alert. A little late.

My muscles clenched, and I bit down the contempt that bubbled up as I crossed the Hall's courtyard toward the front steps.

The *Order*.

I despised the organization. Bureaucratic. Self-righteous. Interfering. They'd been at my heels for decades, trying to take me down any chance they got. I'd made it a personal vendetta to undermine them whenever the opportunity presented itself. And yet here *I* was, offering to help them.

I gritted my teeth. *Oh, how the mighty have fallen.*

I proceeded toward a hastily erected concrete barricade. Three sentries moved to block the entrance. One called for backup, and four or five bluecoats rushed out the front doors and took up positions on the stairs.

My reputation appeared to have preceded me.

Good.

One of the bluecoats stepped out to block my path. I locked him in place with a glare and checked his badge. "Out of my way, Blakely." I poured venom into his name, using it like a verbal cudgel to beat him back. Doubt flickered in the corner of his eyes, so I stepped forward, testing his resolve. He shifted, and his hand fell to the magi-taser at his hip.

I'd snap his arm if he dared use that on me.

"The Hall is locked down. No entry. You need to leave, sir," one of the guards beside Blakely said, aiming for confidence but missing the mark.

"I have information for Detective Cross about the attacks today. Let me pass."

Bolstered by his buddy's air of confidence, Blakely

slammed his hand into my shoulder. "Get back, Fallen. You're not welcome here."

Frustration surged in my veins, and it took all the restraint I had not to instantly break his wrist. I gave a low growl. "Remove your hand."

His sneer ignited my rage. The efreet's power struggled in my soul alongside the dark angel, demanding to be unleashed, and I felt his fury melding with my own.

The efreet was part of me now. I could burn these guards down where they stood. But that would only create more problems, and too much was at stake. This called for precision. I summoned the efreet's magic and focused on Blakely's wristwatch. The metal flared bright orange as its temperature soared. Blakely yelped, released me, and tore at his watch, trying to get it off.

The guards on the steps drew their sidearms and fanned out. "Hands up, Fallen!" one of them shouted.

This was going downhill fast. Despite my powers, I couldn't dodge bullets. These morons were amped up on adrenaline from the attack on Bentham and were going to shoot first and ask question later.

I slowly raised my hands. "I've got information."

One of the bluecoats gestured with his gun. "Kneel and put your hands behind your back."

I didn't have time for this or for his general fucking disposition.

The bluecoats were past the Hall's protective barrier,

so I poured the efreet's magic into their sidearms, instantly heating them a couple hundred degrees.

Guns clattered to the ground around me as trigger-happy goons screamed in surprise.

I liked this new magic.

For the hell of it, I fried their radios, too. I didn't need any more idiots running into the situation half-cocked.

Blakely took a step forward, hand on his taser, and I bared my teeth. "Nobody move. To be clear, I have enough power to kill you all where you stand, but that's not how I want this to go down."

He snorted. One of the bluecoats glanced at the pistol at his feet, calculating. I shook my head. "I wouldn't touch those guns. If I heat them up anymore, they'll explode. And if I see any of you starting to cast, this won't end well for you."

The shifters among the guards were clearly struggling to control their beasts. I got that. I was barely holding back my own demons.

Slowly lowering my hands, I stepped around Blakely and up to the biggest shifter in the group, letting my full signature show. The fallen angel. The ice magic. The efreet's power. I let it overwhelm them.

"This is *my* city. I am here to protect it. I have the name of the man behind this attack, and I'm taking my information upstairs. Grab your nightsticks and follow behind, but I'm going in."

I locked eyes with him and waited until he turned his face away. He knew who was alpha here. The rest would follow.

The sturdy backbone of Magic Side law enforcement melted away as I marched up the stairs. I didn't bother looking back. I could sense the cacophony of magical signatures following behind.

The front doors were locked. "Open it," I barked. I could have done it with a spell in a second—unlocking was my specialty—but I wanted signs of submission. I glared at the shifter. "Now."

He bared his teeth, but after a moment, he signaled someone on the inside.

The door buzzed, then clicked. I pushed it open.

The fucking entry hall was filled with bluecoats, guns drawn.

Gods damn it.

I stared up at the high-domed ceiling and asked for patience, then slowly stepped forward, testing the gunline. "I am bringing in information about the attack."

Safeties clicked off around the room as more cops and curious office staff filtered in the side halls.

That was a lot of guns. They'd probably blow me away if I even started casting a spell.

Visions of reducing the Hall of Inquiry to a molten crater danced in my mind.

Suddenly, a woman's voice echoed through the cavernous entry hall. "Everybody stand *the fuck* down!"

The bluecoats lost their nerve, and most lowered their weapons.

A shifter woman, eyes blazing, stormed across the marble floor. Powerful magic radiated off of her. It tasted like harvest time and smelled like the crisp fall air.

Neve's boss. I'd seen her before when we came back from the Realm of Air. She was bristling and ready to shift.

"What the hell do you think you're doing?" she growled.

I didn't back down. "I'm doing my best to convince your goons not to shoot an unarmed civilian."

"Don't get cute, Malek. Nobody is unarmed in this city, especially you. Word is you assaulted the officers at the gate, and now you're forcing your way onto government property."

"As I told your goons before they jumped me, I have information about today's attacks. But I'll *only* speak with Detective Cross."

I didn't know how much Neve had shared about our working relationship, and I preferred not to give information to the Order if I didn't have to.

"What's your business with Cross?"

I stonewalled her.

The woman stared at me with burning eyes, then sighed. "Come with me, Mr. Malek. And if you pull any of that shit you pulled outside, I'll nail your wings to the Hall's front lintel." She looked over her shoulder. "The rest of you get back to work. This isn't the fucking O.K. Corral."

I followed her down the central hall.

"Name's Lieutenant Mays. Call me Gretchen," she said, not bothering to turn.

We rounded the corner, and I was hit by a force that cranked my nerves to high alert—Neve's signature, coming from the room at the far end of the hall. My pulse quickened, and a sense of relief eased the tension in my shoulders.

She was alive.

"Cross is speaking with Madame DuVoir. Considering who she works for, I'm sure you're already acquainted. If you know anything about the curse or how to stop it, you better share." Gretchen shot me a piercing *don't fuck with me* side glance.

A curse?

"What happened at Bentham?"

"We're assessing." She tossed her hair. "I'm betting you already know most of the details."

Not many, which was infuriating. They must have really locked down on leaks. Rather than betray ignorance, I pivoted. "I heard the Archives flooded."

"Solved. Cross and one of our archmages closed off the breach. Still not sure what blasted through ten feet of reinforced concrete. It was a close call."

Of course Neve would have thrown herself into danger to save a couple of books. Irritation prickled across my skin. Too much risk for ink and paper.

The shifter woman paused, concern flickering in her deep yellow eyes. "Despite showing up like an entitled asshole and setting the whole building off, your help would be appreciated."

I read Gretchen's face as we neared the frosted glass door ahead, shocked at how forthcoming she was, even though—judging from the daggers she kept shooting—she despised me. The feeling was mutual.

Gretchen pushed the door open, and I strode into the crowded office.

8

Neve

I leaned my elbow on my new desk in operations, staring at Ethan and Lily DuVoir, who sat across from me. After returning from Bentham prison, the three of us were discussing ways to break the marid's curse on the prison. According to Lily, we had three days at most to figure this out.

My stomach grumbled, and frustration gnawed at my patience. "Just to be clear, there's no spell that can break the curse on Bentham?"

"Correct," Lily said. "Your only option is to either kill the genie that set the curse or banish it from this world."

I rubbed my temples and sighed. We had two major problems.

One: gods only knew where Matthias and his genies were holed up.

Two: we'd gotten lucky with the efreet. The only reason we were able to defeat him was that Amira and I had pulled him into his contrary plane. That stunt wasn't going to work twice. My stomach twisted at the notion of having to face the djinn and the marid at once, not to mention Matthias. Just the thought of the djinn made my tattoos itch.

I turned to the archmage. "There's got to be another way. Ethan?"

The hairs on my neck suddenly stood on end, and goosebumps danced across my skin.

Damian's signature hit me before I saw him—a pulsing heat that smelled of the ocean, forests, and flames. Not sandalwood, though—he was suppressing that.

My heart clenched as I looked up to meet Damian's blazing eyes with a cold stare. "What the *heck* is he doing here?"

The chatter of voices in the office had stopped, and the room was awkwardly silent. I glanced around the sea of blank faces. At least now my coworkers had someone else to stare at.

"Neve. My office, now." Gretchen said, crossing the room and seemingly unfazed by the presence of the Order's *most wanted* following closely behind.

"What?" I shook my head and stood, utterly confused.

Damian's eyes fell to the wound on my thigh, now healed, then flashed to Ethan. His jaw tightened, and something crossed his face. Rage.

Ethan's magic flared beside me, and I realized that he was having a stare-down with Damian. I looked between them blankly, feeling the tension rising in the room.

What the fates was happening?

Lily scooted her chair back with a screech and gave me a quizzical look.

How was I the only one who wasn't okay with this? All right, maybe Ethan wasn't *okay* with this.

"You want me to go in there with you?" Lily said.

Damian paused at the doorway to Gretchen's office and stared at Ethan and me, fists clenched, aura flickering.

"Thanks. I can handle this one *all* on my own." I picked up my notebook and headed into Gretchen's office, ignoring Damian's burning gaze as I took up a position in the furthest corner of the room.

I couldn't *wait* to hear what this was about.

Gretchen's office was uncomfortably small with the three of us in there, not to mention suffocatingly hot. My skin flushed, and I almost shrugged Rhia's jacket off before thinking better of it. If my coworkers saw my new tattoos, they'd think I was even more of a weirdo.

Gretchen was wearing a blazer and didn't seem bothered by the sudden heat in the room.

I glared at Damian, who stood opposite me, watching me closely, looking deadly and gorgeous. Gods, it was maddening.

And how the heck did he get inside the Hall of Inquiry?

Gretchen shut the door and sat in her leather chair. "Mr. Malek has information concerning the attacks today."

Damian seemed to consider his words before speaking, then began. "Matthias the Iron Mage is responsible for this."

"We already knew that," Gretchen growled.

Damian shot me a deadly stare that sent chills skittering up my spine. He was obviously worried that I'd shared his secrets, and rightfully so.

I crossed my arms and tried to play it cool. "We know Matthias stole the djinn and that he now has a marid. Probably the same one who hit Bentham with the tsunami today."

I had no way of telling Damian that I hadn't spilled the secrets, and I couldn't let Gretchen know that I'd been working with him. Not if I still wanted my job, that is.

Damian nodded, some of his tension easing. "I'll sum things up, then. Matthias is in league with demons and appears to be summoning an army. He's building a new stronghold somewhere. I've seen it. "

Those last words caught me off guard. He'd taken my suggestion earlier in the park seriously and tracked Matthias down.

Fates. That was dangerous.

"Where is this stronghold?" Gretchen asked, concern pulling at the corners of her mouth.

Damian broke his gaze from mine. "I'll tell you all I know. And I'll find him, but only if Ms. Cross agrees to help me hunt him down."

My cheeks blazed with anger. Was he manipulating me into working with him now? When he couldn't get his way by playing fair? *Bastard.*

"I don't know what the hell is going on between the two of you, and I *don't want* to know." Gretchen glared at me and stood. "Frankly, I don't care. We've got three days, tops, to crack this curse before Magic Side is overrun with the worst kind of trouble. Will you work with him, Neve?"

Well, when she put it that way, what other option did I have?

"Fine. I'll work with you," I said bitterly. I couldn't tell if the butterflies in my stomach were from fear or excitement.

"Great. Figure out what's going on and report back to me, personally. I've got a meeting with the head of PR in five. And Neve," she said as Damian and I exited the room, "get him out of here before security sends in a team of enforcers."

They were the Order's black ops team, usually reserved for the highest threat. Considering Damian was standing inside one of the Order's main headquarters, I was surprised they *weren't* there already.

"It'd be my pleasure, L.T." I closed the office door, ignoring Damian's burning stare. "Come on, Mr. Malek."

Neve

Damian, Lily DuVoir, and I made our way along the shaded walkway of Exposition Park.

Lily tugged her cowl forward as I looked back over my shoulder at the swarm of guards in front of the Hall of Inquiry. The last thing I needed was to be seen leaving with Damian Malek—I'd be ostracized forever.

I'd sneaked us out the back entrance because, apparently, Damian had caused some sort of an uproar coming in.

Fates, how much worse was today going to get?

I probably shouldn't ask.

I glared at Damian. "You said you visited Matthias's stronghold. Where is it?"

"I was hoping you could tell me." Damian handed

me his phone, and my fingers brushed his. "This must be the portal he used to move his army from the Searing Citadel."

Ignoring the arc of energy that shot through my palm, I glanced down at the picture—a circle of runes— and frowned, then handed the phone to Lily. "You actually went through this portal?"

"No. It was closed. But while I was there, the citadel was teleported somewhere. It's no longer in the Realm of Fire."

"You're telling me Matthias teleported the entire citadel to another realm?" A tightness clenched my chest as I calculated how much power that would have required. Infinite. The Searing Citadel was a massive construction hewn out of stone. "Do you know which realm he moved it to?"

Damian's intense gaze sent shivers across my skin. "Not sure. I've only got photos of the runes."

Lily's brows pinched together as she scrutinized the screen, and then she handed the phone back to Damian. "I'm not sure. I recognize a few, but I have no idea where it would lead."

Damian cursed under his breath.

"But," she continued, "perhaps I can help you share your memories of this place with Neve. We'll need to do it at my place, though."

I looked between Lily and Damian. "Let's do it."

9

Neve

Fifteen minutes later, we pulled up in front of Lily's redbrick apartment in the Dockside Dens—a neighborhood down by the old freighter docks that was run by Magic Side's criminal underground, popularly known as the Underworld.

I stepped out of Damian's car and glanced up at the building's art deco tower. Last time I'd visited Lily's place, I'd been run out by a mob of marsh men. Hopefully, this time would go differently.

A couple of rough-looking shifters tracked our movements from across the street. I kept my head down, hoping they wouldn't recognize me. With Damian at my side, they would think twice about causing trouble, but I didn't want to get a reputation for poking my nose in places it didn't belong.

Well, *more* of a reputation.

Lily glided up the front steps, pulling a set of keys from her pocket. "This won't take long."

I glanced at my phone—four-thirty p.m.

Damian stepped to the side, gesturing for me to go ahead. He was so freaking polite sometimes, it made me nauseous. I knew the truth behind his façade.

The stairwell smelled of cinnamon and vanilla—cookies? My stomach growled as we reached the first-floor landing. I inspected the deep red wallpaper that decorated the lower half of the walls. The last time I was here, I'd entered from the building's fire escape.

Lily unlocked her front door with a *snick* and stepped aside so we could enter. "Please come in."

The warm lights of her apartment flared to life with the flick of her wrist. I recognized the Bohemian decor, but the vintage green couch in the corner was a new addition.

Lily shucked her coat on a chair and glided into the adjoining room. "You two can sit in here. I'll just gather a few things."

I took a seat at the round table in the center of the room. Damian followed and took the closest chair to mine. I gave a pointed glance at the three other unoccupied chairs, trying to ignore how his magic prickled my skin—in the *best* way imaginable. Did he have to sit so close? It was bad enough I had to work with him. I shouldn't have to bask in his signature.

He had a darkness inside of him, and half of his aura was stolen magic. One day, it might include mine. I shouldn't be relishing the scent of forests and the sound of the sea.

But I was.

And that pissed me the heck off.

Damian's aura was even stronger now, and I could sense the efreet's magic in him—the scent of burning incense and the crackle of flames. I focused on those, and the terrible memories they brought, trying to drown out the rest.

It didn't really work.

Lily drifted back into the room with an almost eerie grace. Her arms were full of books and bobbles, which she dumped on the back workbench and began to sort through. She looked over her shoulder at Damian. "The citadel was in the Realm of Fire before it was teleported somewhere else, correct?"

"Correct."

She nodded and slid an orange crystal ball under her arm, then grabbed a candle and a handful of some kind of dried herbs from a shelf at the far side of the room. She deposited the herbs in the center of the table and set the crystal and candle between Damian and me. "You two must place your right hands together."

My back went rigid, and my gaze shot to hers. "Is that a requirement or a suggestion?"

I really didn't want to touch him. His signature made my head spin and stirred feelings inside me that were... uncomfortable and downright dirty. Did I mention dangerous?

Lily raised a brow and pulled a silk ribbon from her pocket. "A requirement, love."

I sighed and shifted my chair toward Damian, placing my right elbow on the table like we were about to have an arm-wrestling match. He placed his elbow beside mine and took my hand in his. My muscles tensed as warmth cascaded into my palm, winding its way up my arm and into my chest. I tried to steady my breathing, but my heart thudded like a freaking jackhammer.

"Perfect." Lily came around the table and wound the ribbon around our wrists.

I glared at Damian and noticed something flash across his perfect face. Amusement?

Lily lit the candle and took a seat opposite us. "Now, both of you close your eyes. Damian, focus on the memory you want to share. Neve, you must open your-self up to him."

Like *heck* I would. Did she know he was a FireSoul? Of course not—she would never have invited him in.

I closed my eyes and took a breath, trying to calm my mind and the panic that seeped into my veins. I'd only open myself up a little. Just enough to see this memory.

Lily whispered an incantation, and a burst of energy exploded around us. The smell of burnt rose and oleander infiltrated my nose. I peeked open an eye and squinted at the sharp light. The crystal ball between us was glowing like a sun, and the pile of dried herbs had turned to ash. Lily's palms were face down on the table, her eyes open but solid white. "Focus."

I closed my eye and willed myself to focus.

Five seconds passed, and I began to feel something —the slightest tug at my consciousness, like I was about to fall into a deep sleep. Suddenly, magic flooded me, rivers dragging my mind through memories I couldn't place. Then it stopped, and a vision appeared in the distance, bathed in orange light. I walked through the darkness toward it, and recognition dawned—it was a room in the Searing Citadel.

A rush of warm air hit me as I stepped into the domed chamber. I saw Damian, standing before a circle of runes, like a god born out of the flames. Then the memory became like a dream, hazy, and soft around the edges. Like moving, but being trapped in a body you had no control over.

A flood of magic suddenly rocked the room and threw me—Damian, *us*—to the ground. Pain convulsed through me as the cosmos swirled, threatening to tear me to pieces.

Damian must have planes-walked.

Pain surged through my body, and I jolted in the chair. Damian's grip on my hand tightened, towing a part of me back to reality. This was just a vision—a memory of his—but it felt so *real*.

Then I was back in it. The spinning had stopped, and we were in the citadel.

Damian raced up a stairwell, his blade in hand, now lit with fire. Hunting.

He slammed his shoulder into a massive iron door and pushed his way onto a balcony.

I gasped as brutally cold air cut my skin.

Everything was wrong. This was not the Realm of Fire.

I searched for the lava lake, but it was gone. Instead, the citadel sat upon a massive island of ice, floating in a purple sky. Magic runes blazed around the base.

The four suns were also gone. Instead, the sky was like a nebula, a vast expanse of swirling, unearthly clouds that cast a purple light across the world.

I could sense the deep magical signature of the place through Damian's memory. Everything about it felt off, as if *it* didn't even know what it was.

Where was this world?

A demonic host circled in the air. Their magic overwhelmed my senses. There were too many smells, tastes, sounds. Many signatures were weak, but some radiated power.

And then, on a floating chunk of ice, there was Matthias. And the djinn. And the marid.

They were weaving spells with the demons.

Fates.

The djinn looked up at me and grinned.

Rage colored my vision, and I felt the storm rise within me.

Suddenly, a ball of fire enveloped me, burning my skin.

I gasped as the vision crumbled and reality crashed into me. Damian gripped my shoulder, and I opened my eyes, relief filling me when I recognized Lily's apartment. A bead of sweat rolled down my neck, and my skin felt clammy.

"Are you all right?" Damian looked at me, concern in his darkened eyes.

Lily appeared beside us and quickly unwound the ribbon from our wrists. "I'm sorry. That wasn't supposed to happen like that." She paused, then crossed to the shelf of crystals.

Damian leaned back in his chair, worry etched on his face.

Fear iced me. "What do you mean? How *exactly* was that supposed to happen?"

Lily turned, her brows knit together. "Usually, you just see the memory. But for some reason, you felt it. Like you and Damian had melded into one. That shouldn't happen. It's very dangerous."

She looked visibly distraught, and that scared the heck out of me.

"Okay. So we won't do *that* again," I said.

Damian scrubbed a hand through his hair and stood, crossing to the window.

Lily handed us each a glass of iced tea. "Did you learn anything from the memory?"

I took a sip. It was cool and refreshing, and my mouth was parched. "Wherever Matthias teleported the citadel, it isn't in the Realm of Air, that's for certain. The tower was floating, but the signature of the place was all wrong."

I shivered. I'd never felt anything like the magic in that place. It was confused, noisy, and almost maddening, like an orchestra playing many songs at once.

Damian turned, locking me with an intense gaze that sent tingles up my thighs. What the heck? My cheeks burned, and flames danced in his eyes. Judging from the expression on his face, he felt it, too.

Lily's voice broke the silence. "Any clues that might indicate where it might be?"

I blinked twice and tore my eyes from Damian. "I've been to the Realms of Water and Fire, and it wasn't one of those. And I think I'd recognize the Realm of Earth, as I've felt its signature before, which is terrible, by the way. This place was somewhere strange and unnatural. I need to think."

"Hm. I guess the question is, then, what is Matthias doing, and why put a curse on the prison?" Lily said.

Damian lowered his glass, his face solemn. "I think he's preparing for war."

Silence filled the room.

I frowned. "Against whom? The Order?"

He shook his head. "The Watchers. Our ancient adversary."

My heart sank, and dread filled me. The Watchers were an order of angels that watched over earth. If Matthias was raising a demon army and planned to go to war against them, Magica and humanity would be caught in the crossfire.

Lily appeared to feel the same. She'd sunk into a chair, seemingly lost in thought. "Well, you better figure out where this stronghold is and stop him. You've got two to three days before the curse devours the prison's protective wards and Bentham's criminals join Matthias's cause."

I anxiously rubbed the opal around my neck. "We need more clues. Heck, *any* clues would be nice."

Damian shook his head. "Matthias is clever enough to cover his tracks. I went to his house, but he burned it to the ground when he split town. Do you think your friend Rhiannon could sense anything there?"

Matthias's house. That pinged something at the back of my mind.

"Zara," I whispered. "Matthias's assistant." I didn't know why I hadn't thought of her before.

"You're right." Damian crossed to the table and set his glass down. "We must find her."

I pulled out my phone and dialed Gretchen. She picked up on the second ring. "Hi, L.T.," I began. "Still no progress on Matthias. I want to bring in his assistant for questioning. Can you get me a warrant?"

Gretchen agreed immediately, and I hung up and looked to Damian. "Any ideas on where she might be?"

"No, but I'll find her."

Lily stood and smiled warmly. "I wish you both the best of luck. Let me know if I can be of further assistance."

As Damian and I walked to the door, she placed her hand on my elbow, motioning for me to stop.

"One more thing, Neve," she whispered, glancing at Damian, who was in the other room. "I have the power of true sight and know what you are. I sensed it the first time we met. But your power is growing. Be careful. Power can be a curse. If you transition to a full djinn, you can be bound and forced to use your magic against your will."

Her words froze me. *Bound.* That was what people did to genies—bound them to magical objects and extorted wishes from them. It was the reason I'd hidden my heritage for so long.

I'd die before I let someone force me to use my power against my will.

"I'll never let that happen." I meant both things—becoming a full djinn *and* being bound.

I stepped into the foyer and glanced at Damian, who'd turned his back to me. He'd stopped, and his body was rigid.

Fates, had he heard that?

The floor creaked. As if stirred from a daze, his body relaxed, and he continued to the door.

10

Damian

I opened the passenger door, and Neve gracefully slipped into the Corvette. I dropped into the driver's side, turned the key, and sped north through town.

Neve shot me a tentative look. "You can feel Zara? With your...powers?"

I nodded. I could find what I wanted using my dragon sense. The object of my desire was like a string tugging on my gut, pulling me in its direction.

Neve was doing that all of the time these days. Sharing my memory with her had only made it worse.

I tried to focus on Zara, but it was difficult. I'd only met her once, and Neve's pull on me nearly drowned everything else out.

And Neve was in danger. I'd heard what Lily said—that Neve could be bound, just like we'd bound the djinn in the Realm of Air. I could never let that happen to her. Would she become a true djinn if she granted a wish? That had nearly happened to her a week ago in some bar. A silly accident and a very close call.

I'd have to be vigilant.

The city lights raced by as I silently brooded on her situation. Neve was uncharacteristically quiet, and I guessed she was pondering the same thing.

Zara's signature tugged at me, and I turned east and out onto the Midway, trying to avoid the relentless stop signs of cross-town traffic. She was somewhere in the Midway Dens, one of the more chaotic portions of the city. It was run by demons and devils, though all kinds of people lived there—mostly people who didn't like being told what to do. I knew the Midway Boss well. He was hands-off as long as he got a cut and wouldn't give us any trouble. Hell, I'd been boxing in one of his favorite spots for the last few days and was becoming a bit of a local.

"Earlier, you said that the Watchers were your enemy. Is that because..." Neve paused. "Because they kicked you out of heaven?"

The memories of my fall, of aligning with Matthias, and our war against the heavens were like a twisted dagger in my heart. I'd locked them away in the furthest recesses of my mind, but recently, they'd come flooding back.

"One of many reasons." I glanced at Neve. The streetlights cast a warm glow on her skin. Another dagger twisted into my heart.

We skidded through a junction just before the light turned and roared north on Razorback Avenue. Small brick-built shops lined the streets, apothecaries to dressmakers to sex shops. Neve drummed her fingers on the glass. "Wow. To be honest, I haven't spent much time over here. I think I've been missing out. At least on the clothes. Look at the fabulous boots on that...individual."

I tightened my lips to hold back a smile. "The Midway Dens are a real cornucopia of delights."

Zara's signature peaked as we passed a black brick building with windows made of dark glass cubes. I slammed on the brakes and backed quickly into a spot. Furious honking erupted from the car behind me.

I slipped out and opened the door for Neve. "This is it."

Neve gave the building a skeptical look. An animated neon sign of a she-devil danced above the door. Blinking letters below advertised *The Rift*.

She bit her lip slightly. "This is going to be interesting."

A hulking, blue-skinned demon with a huge rack of horns lounged beside the doorway. His magic felt like an earthquake and tasted like soot and cayenne. He shifted his frame to block the door as we tried to push our way through.

"Not welcome," the demon snapped.

I locked him with a piercing gaze. "Damian Malek."

The bouncer ground his teeth but pushed the door open.

"They know you here?" Neve whispered.

"No. They know me everywhere."

The bar was dark and smoky and lit by feeble red lights, and half the patrons stopped talking as soon as we stepped in. Demons, devils, shifters—it was a dangerous crowd tonight. Probably every night. We caught dirty stares from some, but most went back to talking.

Unease radiated off of Neve, and I gave her a knowing smile. "Don't worry. You could take this place on your own." I didn't doubt it, considering what she'd done to her neighborhood while fighting the efreet.

The Rift was a real dive, and a popular one at that. The long bar top was packed shoulder to shoulder and horn to horn. The fiendish folk were playing dice games and watching NASCAR on a couple of TVs hanging from the ceiling. A single glance at the top shelf told me they had a hell of a whiskey selection. I'd have to keep that in mind.

The bartender was a true demon—second or third circle—with massive, curled horns and glowing tattoos. You didn't see many of those around. The sound of his magic cracked like lightning bolts and felt like a sandstorm. He raised an eyebrow, but I shook my head and started pushing through the packed bodies. Sardines from hell.

"Where is she?" Neve shouted in my ear, trying to speak over the din of the crowd and the local blues rock band.

It was hard to see much in the low light, but Zara was here. Close.

"Somewhere in the back."

We didn't have to shove our way through for long. I flexed my aura, and people quickly cleared a path.

The walls were plastered with Polaroid photos of people and their cars. Hell, I hadn't realized they made Polaroids anymore.

A chalkboard with *Menu* on the top hung on the far wall. It listed one item in capital blue letters: <u>*MEATS*</u>. That explained why the smoky scent of BBQ permeated the place.

The throng thinned out toward the back. There were a couple of professional dancers, but they seemed mainly in it for themselves.

Neve widened her eyes...but then we caught sight of Zara.

She was at a round wooden table playing poker with a couple of demons. The tabletop was covered with graffiti and so many poorly carved runes, I was surprised it didn't explode in a fireball of uncontrolled magic.

Everybody had their horns out. Zara's were short and poked up through her purple-highlighted hair. Her black-lined eyes flashed my way, and she uttered an inaudible curse. Catching herself, she put on a sardonic smile. "Mulder and Scully. What a pleasant surprise."

"Zara. We need to talk," I said.

"Great. I'm sure this will be riveting. Pull up a chair. Please tell me they're reopening the X-Files." She tossed back a shot of tequila and put the glass upside down on the table.

Walking up, I caught three players' hands in a single glimpse. One hand bluffing, the next deuces...and, well, the third was either a bad hand or belonged to someone who didn't understand how to play. I could clean these dupes out with my eyes shut.

"We should talk in private," I said as softly as I could in the noisy bar.

"Nah, I prefer it here." She swept her hand out, indicating the blues band, the dancers, and the bar. In a single whimsical gesture, she twisted a finger. "I'm trying to unwind."

"We need you to answer some questions about Matthias. I doubt you want to talk about that in company," Neve said.

Zara looked from me to Neve. "Who's asking, Damian Malek or the Order?"

"Both," I said.

"Yeah. Then no. Twice."

Her demon pal laughed, shot tequila out his nose, and started choking.

Neve pushed past me. "Zara, some serious shit is going down. We need to know where Matthias is."

"Don't know. Don't care."

I tapped on the tabletop, looked at the runes, and thought better of it. "I find both of those things hard to believe."

"I find it hard to believe that the two of you would come into this place and try to shake me down. Beat it." Zara reached for a card.

Neve slammed her hand on the deck, magic crackling along her tattoos and at the corner of her eyes. "Cut the bullshit, Zara. Magic Side is at risk. Matthias is responsible for the attack on Old Mud City."

Zara smiled and tugged at the card under Neve's hand. It didn't come off the deck. "I heard it was an efreet. And a djinn."

"An efreet under his control," Neve hissed.

Zara gave up trying to pull the card. "Prove it. I heard it was the Smoking Man. He's behind everything."

Neve gave a low growl, her patience nearly spent. "I'm not messing around here, Zara. Matthias's minions attacked the Archives today, *and* Bentham. As we speak, shit is going down, and if we don't do something, this city is going to be overrun with murderers and thieves. Do you seriously want Magic Side burned to the ground and everyone in Bentham running free?"

"Woo! Free Reggie!" a demon hollered from somewhere off to the side.

A cluster of patrons took up the chant, pounding the tabletop. "Free Reggie! Free Reggie!"

I had no idea who Reggie was, but this was not going well. We were making the wrong arguments in the wrong place to the wrong people.

I turned to Neve, but a woman in a sporty racing jacket barged through. "What's going on, Zara? Who are these creeps?"

She was a half-devil sporting curled horns and long, dark hair. She flicked her pointed tail back and forth in agitation.

Zara grinned. "Hey, Rayne. They're from the FBI. They investigate aliens."

The she-devil—her name pronounced like rain—furrowed her brow. "What?"

Neve slammed her fist into the table, spilling tequila everywhere. "Fates be damned, Zara, we need help."

"Back off," the she-devil snapped, shoving close to Neve. I shot my arm between them, but Neve's aura surged as her fury rose. Wind whipped around her, and she rose a few inches off the ground.

Zara's eyes darted to Neve's feet and back up. I put my hand on Neve's shoulder to calm her down and push her back to the ground. "Come on, they're not talking. We've got other avenues to explore."

"No, we don't," Neve said and doubled down, locking

eyes with the purple-haired half-demon. "Tell us where Matthias is and what he's up to, or we'll drag you downtown and ask you some less than friendly questions."

A dozen chairs scraped on the old wooden floor as demons and devils all around us stood.

I dropped my hand to my side, ready to summon my blade. Neve would fight to protect her city, and I would fight to protect her.

I spun at the sound of a steel blade slowly sliding out of a sheath.

A suit of armor loomed over us, its longsword held menacingly in a fighting stance. It was an empty suit animated by Zara's magic. No one was inside.

Zara confidently clucked her tongue. "Now, Bertie, don't be so eager. We needn't go beheading anyone. We're all friends here, aren't we?"

This was getting out of control. Not the way I liked to play my hand.

I nodded at Zara and shot Neve a look. *Diffuse.*

Neve sucked in a breath of air. She often held it when she was agitated. Her aura subsided as she forced her anger down. "Sorry, Zara. We're just worried about the city. This is bigger than any one of us. We've got less than three days before all hell breaks loose."

Zara sighed. "Look, I'm sorry. I don't know anything. Really. I wish you luck in your investigation. Have a couple shots on the way out."

She poured us a couple of tequilas.

Neve grabbed her wrist gently and whispered, "Please. You know something. I can sense it."

Fire shot to Zara's eyes as her composure finally snapped. "Damnit, I wish you would just shut up already and go to hell!"

Neve rocked back and gasped as if she'd been slapped in the face. Her tattoos glowed, and then the room began to spin.

11

Neve

Magic surged through my veins like wildfire, burning me from the inside out. I cried out in agony as I tried to fight it down.

Oh, no. I knew what was happening.

Zara made a wish.

The world wheeled around me as I fought to gain control over my magic.

I didn't choose this.

I didn't *want* this.

Unimaginable power raced through me, demanding to be released. The world flickered, the walls of the bar melting. Flames rose around us on all sides.

Everyone panicked. Patrons leapt from their seats.

Demons staggered into each other as pandemonium exploded through the bar, and flames erupted around us.

I was literally sending the entire bar *to hell*.

Damian grasped my arm. "Fight it, Neve."

I ground my teeth as the magic lashed around inside me like a wild animal. Amid the chaos and screaming, Damian's voice was my rock. "You are the master of your power. It does not control you. It's yours to command. Close your eyes. Grasp the magic. Bend it to your will. You can do this."

I squeezed my eyes shut. The wish pulled against my heart, demanding freedom, but I focused on the bar in my mind. The bar as it *was*. Not in hell, but full of music and drinking and dancing.

Everything shook.

My soul pushed against the magic, forcing it down.

Damian's aura wrapped around me, pouring strength into me. The scent of ancient forests surrounded me. Ocean waves cascaded through my body. The taste of salt crept across my tongue, as if we'd kissed after diving beneath the waves. His warmth spiraled through my body, tickling my skin, and I gasped.

I opened my eyes and realized that I was standing in the middle of the room.

Damian's hand was only touching my arm. Fates, it had felt like more.

People milled about in confusion, picking up personal possessions.

Thank the gods, no one was looking at us except Zara, her half-devil friend, and their posse.

And the bartender.

Shit.

Zara's eyes widened with terror. "What the hells did you just do?"

My gut wrenched.

I nearly sent us all to hell, that's what.

I couldn't control my magic. That was beyond dangerous for a normal Magica. How much more destructive would I become as a full djinn?

I'd be slapped in magicuffs for life, my powers locked down forever. I could never let that happen.

The room reeled.

Be calm. Appear in control. I had to make Zara and her cronies think that little stunt I just pulled was deliberate. I fixed her with an icy stare. "I gave you a taste of what I can do. Be careful what you wish for."

She gaped. "Holy..."

"Hey!" The demonic bartender's voice shook the room. "I don't know what the hell that was, but y'all need to take this outside." Zara started to protest, but the bartender interrupted. "Read the sign and get out. Don't come back until y'all cool off. Tomorrow." He pointed to a large plaque on the wall:

No Killing.
No Snitching.
No Whining.
No Cursing (Magical), Swearing OK

Zara cursed and made for the exit with her posse in tow. She shouldered me on the way out.

Brat.

Sporty Spice, her half-devil friend, groaned. "I just got here! I had a long day at work! It was shots o'clock!"

The bartender would have none of it.

We all shuffled outside. Damian cleared a path with his eyes, and I followed, chants of "Free Reggie" nipping at my heels.

Who the heck was Reggie? Probably some local favorite chained up in Bentham.

Fates. This had gone tits up.

The cool, summer night air hit me like an ocean wave, and I felt my fury drain away. I knew better than to get in Zara's face like that on her turf. What had happened to me? Where was this anger coming from?

My tattoos still tingled. It was all connected. My power. My rage.

I didn't like what I was becoming.

Zara shot daggers at me with her eyes as Damian unlocked the Corvette.

Sporty Spice gave a low whistle and sauntered up, twitching her tail. "Damn. Nice ride."

Damian nodded. "She moves."

The long-haired girl traced the tip of her tail lightly against the hood. "I bet she does."

Jealously sparked—no, *burned*.

Back off, she-devil.

Why the hell did I even care? Take the hussie for a ride.

Zara popped some gum in her mouth and cocked her head. "Come on, Rayne. Let's get out of here."

I took a step toward her. "Please. I don't know what you and Matthias are wrapped up in, but it's bad. If you're worried or not safe, come with us. Shit is going to go down, and this city is going to go up in flames unless we do something. Please help."

She growled and tossed her hair. "Fine. Here's the deal. We settle this our way. You race our team. Damian in the 'vette versus Rayne in our rig. He wins, I come and talk. She wins, you leave us all alone."

I scowled.

The difference between demons and devils was the differences between anarchists and lawyers. Demons loved chaos. Devils loved twisting the rules. Half demons and half devils, like these girls, often had the same tendencies—though not always.

Zara was half demon. I trusted her as far as I could throw her.

I would have rather made a deal with a devil. They could usually be trusted to keep the promises they couldn't weasel out of. Demons, on the other hand... well, you'd better make a blood oath or no deal at all.

But what choice did I have? Dragging her downtown wouldn't make her talk, and we didn't have anything on her. Yet.

I looked at the Corvette and met Damian's eyes. The corner of his mouth ticked up in a confident half smile.

I glanced at Zara. She shot me a pleading, *help a girl out here* look.

Confusion shot through me.

Oh, what the hell. I shrugged. "What's the course?"

Zara made a triangle with her fingers "Dockside run. West up the Midway, down the Diagonal South through Dockside, and back north along Razorback."

This was idiotic.

I turned back to Damian to say as much, but he had fire in his eyes. He wanted this. Was burning for it.

Whatever. We were running out of time and options, and I crossed my arms. "Fine. Damian wins, you tell us what we want to know. She-devil wins, and we leave you alone."

The half devil rolled her eyes and flicked her tail. "It's Rayne."

"Deal." Zara shot out her hand, and I grasped it.

What were we getting into?

12

Neve

The giant bouncer shoved the door open. "Race!"

The *entire* bar emptied, until there was no standing room left along the sidewalk. Folks who couldn't see clambered up on top of cars and dumpsters.

Holy crap.

I put two and two together. All the photos on the walls—this was a street racing club.

Beers and booze in hand, the milling crowd started chanting, "Rayne, Rayne, make it Rayne!"

Oh, fates damn it.

Rayne pulled her Subaru up to the curb with a screech. It was like something out of *Tron*, lit up with pink and teal lights. Zara grinned, flipped up the hood, and fiddled around.

A grease monkey?

I sidled up to Damian. "Uh..."

He grinned. "I've got this. I've got the 'vette."

"And if she doesn't talk after you, uh, probably win?"

"You bring her in with a warrant or figure out a new plan."

"This is all super illegal and dangerous."

Damian shrugged and leaned back on his car. "Welcome to the dark side. It's way more fun."

Damn, he was hot. I could practically taste the confidence oozing off him. His aura surged, and it gave me a shiver.

Bad Neve.

Sporty Spice sauntered over and shot out her hip. "I bet you have some pretty pricey enchantments on that ride."

Damian shrugged. "A few."

"So do we. You want to run clean? I have anti-magic charms. They clip right down on the hood," Sporty said.

"Your course, your rules."

She tossed the charms to her crew. "Cool. As is."

Ten minutes later, everyone was ready to go.

Damian looked like an assassin behind the wheel. My heart pounded in my ears, and I crossed my fingers.

Please, fates, let him win.

Bracing my shoulder on the roof, I leaned into Damian's open window. "Be careful. People die doing this."

"Don't worry."

I did.

I didn't want him around me, but I sure as heck didn't want him dead. He'd been my ally through all of this...even if he was a FireSoul and might kill me and steal my powers.

I bit my lip. This was all sorts of effed up.

The bartender had come out as well, though I don't know how he had fit through the door with that massive rack of horns. He seemed to be the master of ceremonies. With a cacophonous boom, he released a spell that morphed into a burning dragon. It shot off down the racetrack, bellowing, "Get out of the road, racers coming through!"

Zara, leaning against a car beside me, cocked her head. "The spell knows the route. Gives people fair warning, forces them to pull over."

Right. Because a crash at these speeds could be fatal.

This was insane. Thank fates for the dragon spell.

The thrill of combat burned in Damian's eyes. I hadn't ever seen him so charged...or excited. He tightened his grip on the wheel.

A flicker of desire tugged at me, but I snuffed it out. *No way.*

Rayne revved her engine, and Damian's car echoed the sound. The powerful motors shook the ground around us.

The bartender dropped his hands, and the cars screamed down the road, belching exhaust behind them. A roar erupted from the crowd as people shot magic into the air and hurled beer bottles at the wall.

Holy shit, this is crazy.

Zara unleashed her wide, leather wings, gave me a wicked smile, and leapt into the air. "Sucker."

Her friends cheered in approval.

The little hussy! Was she running?

I rocketed up after her as she soared through the sky. No chance that she was going to get away. She was on wings while I was burning magic like jet fuel.

I was on her in seconds.

"Zara, you cheat!" I swiped at her wrist, but she spiraled away, cursing.

"Holy crap, you're fast!"

She dove just out of reach but didn't have my reflexes.

Zara waved her hands as I came at her again. "Back off, I'm going to talk. Why the hell else do you think we're up here?"

"What?"

"Seriously, Scully?" She rolled her eyes. "You expect me to give up my own father in a bar, in front of my crew, in front of half of Magic Side?"

My stomach churned. Of course. It was obvious now —Matthias was her father. To me, he was the enemy. "I..."

"Geez." She sighed. "You don't handle informants ever, do you?"

I shook my head, blood rushing to my face.

"Come on, we gotta sell this. Let's chase the cars," Zara said, and dove in pursuit.

Damian had shot out fast and was ripping down the Midway. Rayne was on him, engine screaming.

I dug my nails into my palms, trying to steady my breathing.

Zara spun toward me. "Look, I don't know much, but I'll tell you what I do know. I don't want this city to burn, either. This is my home. Matthias has changed over the last month. I think he's tied up with some seriously bad people."

"Thanks." I recalled them yelling back and forth in the hall at his house. "And I'm sorry. I can't imagine how hard this must be."

Zara clamped her mouth shut.

Tires shrieked as Damian swung around the hairpin turn onto the Diagonal, leaving black streaks on the pavement. Rayne drifted around the curve like she was on ice and recovered with a burst of speed. In a blink, she was ahead.

Zara sank her nails into my arm. "Matthias has really fucked up. He's drunk on power and doing fucking stupid things, and it's going to get him killed. If I help you, you have to promise me that you'll let him live. You're a cop, right? You'll make sure the Order, the Fallen, or anyone else doesn't hurt him?"

My gut clenched. Could I promise that? "Zara…"

"Promise me. I need your help. You can make that happen. He can't die."

We jetted south, trying to head off the racers as they disappeared down the Diagonal.

I rubbed my pendant. Man, this was a stupid thing to promise.

Rage shadowed Zara's face. She was fighting down tears with anger.

I needed her help. Now she needed mine.

Stop Matthias. Save Matthias. Save the city. Easy.

Fates.

I stuck out my hand. "I'll do it."

She nodded. "I need your oath. We'll do this the demon way."

Zara slipped a knife out of her boot and cut a deep gash across her palm. "I make an oath to tell you what I know about Matthias's plans if you make an oath not to kill him and bring him in alive."

She flew over, tossed me the knife, and held out her bloody palm.

Crap. A demon oath. Break it, and you'd be cursed. At least I'd know she wasn't lying.

I drew the knife across my palm. Its sting left a line of red blood in its wake. My stomach kinda curdled. It was having a rough night.

I slapped my palm into Zara's hand, and we shook.

Demonic magic burned through my veins as the blood in my palm boiled, searing my skin.

I reeled. Holy fates, that was strong stuff.

Zara grinned. "First time?"

"Yep. Hopefully, the last."

We circled through the sky back to Razorback Avenue. No way we would catch up with them on the Diagonal. They were totally out of sight.

Zara turned to face me as we flew. "Matthias is building a new realm, like the Realm of Air. But this time, it's a Realm of Chaos. I saw some of his spells and designs. He's using the genies to shape the elements to create a new world that he will rule for eternity."

Holy shit. I'd suspected something like that, but to hear it confirmed...

"That explains a lot. Is he there?"

"Probably," she said.

"I think Damian was accidently transported there. Matthias is assembling a demon army. What do you know about it?"

"Nothing. I'm not part of those plans. I told you he's into some bad shit. Through all the wars, I guess he got tied up with some fiends."

My heart raced. "How do we stop him?"

"The genies have already woven the spells binding the elements of fire, water, and air. He's missing an earth genie. The world won't be stable without its spells."

Okay. That was something. My mind started ticking. "Anything else?"

"The spells are consuming far more energy than he anticipated. He tried to get me to work the math, but, well, it's not a strength."

"So what will he do?"

"He mentioned a city somewhere around the Black Sea...Apollonia Parva or something like that. It's in ruins. But there are some old artifacts there that serve as batteries to power the invisibility spells that shroud it. Like the ones that conceal Guild City and Magic Side."

I could use that. Somehow. This was good.

We shot out over Razorback Avenue. The cars were screaming up the road, neck and neck.

I whipped out my phone and dialed Damian. I knew it would ring through to his car.

"Fates, Neve, I'm racing! What?" he growled.

"Let her win."

"Are you kidding?"

"I got what I need. Zara, Matthias's *daughter*, needs to save face."

He hung up.

I shrugged at Zara. "He doesn't like losing, I don't think."

Zara scrunched up her brow. "Who does?"

13

The Rift

Damian

I shoved the pedal down, and the Corvette screamed past the cars parked along Razorback Avenue. The street was ours, a straight shot to the finish.

A fake finish.

Irritation burned though my veins, and I dug my fingers into the wheel.

Lose.

Intentionally.

The absolute gall of it.

This would have been a tight race either way, but at least I would have had my pride.

I eased off the gas a fraction as I chased Rayne's taillights. She was good, brilliant. Like a skater on ice. She deserved a fair win. Or loss.

What a day. First, I was jumping at Neve's beck and call. Then I was working with the Order. Now, I was throwing a race.

Fates, what was I becoming? I didn't like it one bit.

I cursed and hit the accelerator, trying to overtake the Subaru. Rayne drifted left, as if reading my mind.

Damnit.

I tried to ease off, but it burned at everything I was.

"This is why no one in their right mind makes a deal with a demon," I said to the Corvette. "Halfway through, they change the rules."

Matthias taught me that long ago. Apparently, his daughter was no different.

I cursed my short-sightedness. I should have known. There was a little similarity in their signatures, but I'd just assumed that she was one of his apprentices. He'd had plenty of those. For as long as I'd known Matthias, he had despised the idea of creating a true progeny.

He'd definitely changed. What had happened?

I swerved to dodge a giant pothole, frustration rumbling in my chest. "What the hell is wrong with the Magic Side Department of Transportation?"

My poor Corvette wondered the same thing, I was sure.

I sucked a breath through my clenched teeth and tried

to stifle my irritation. Somehow, Neve had gotten the information we needed. That was important—the long game. If losing was part of the deal, then I could live with it.

I'd thrown card games before when trying to work a mark. The loss was the win. You had to play your hand right to make it convincing. Was this any different?

Yes.

Rayne pulled ahead in a sudden jet of speed and shot across the Midway intersection, crossing the finish line in a puff of magic.

Where did that boost come from?

Hell. She probably had some more tricks up her sleeve. She was a devil and probably used to racing dirty. That's how they played the game here.

I slammed on my brakes, and the 'vette swerved over the finish. I brought her to a stop in the middle of the street.

Rayne slid out of the driver's seat and was mobbed by the denizens of the Midway Den.

Time to face the music. I sighed and got out.

The crowd was hooting and hollering and chanting, "Make it Rayne!" A couple of revelers shook my hand as a cluster formed around the 'vette.

A nerdy blue demon with thick glasses reached his claws out toward the car. "Hey kid," I snapped. "No touching."

He gave an apologetic grin and pulled back.

That's right.

Zara dropped out of the sky, ran over to the car, and gave it a quick once over. She turned and shouted at Rayne, "Tell me you didn't rough up my baby."

"She's fine. It was an easy run."

Irritation pricked my skin.

A blunt force slammed into my back, followed by the crackle of lightning and a rush of magic that felt like a sandstorm. The meaty hand of the demon bartender wrapped around my shoulder. "Fallen! You made my night. This was a good run! Here." He shoved a whiskey bottle into my hand. "Drink."

What the hell. I kicked back the bottle.

Damn. That was smooth. What was I drinking?

I checked the label. Impressive.

"Special for you," the horned bartender said. "You did well. Come back anytime you wish. I'm sorry I kicked you out, but it worked out okay."

I shook his hand, feeling a little better about events. "Okay."

He clapped me on the back and started to walk away. "Also, loser buys drinks for the bar. I'll set up a tab."

Of course they did. I shrugged. "Fine. I'm good for it."

"I know. Come race any time." He waved at the crowd. "Drinks on Malek."

They roared and mobbed me.

I disentangled myself from the crush of horns and wings and tails and found Neve by the Subaru.

Rayne punched me in the arm. "That was fun. Real close, there. We should do this again."

I glared at her. "Never touch me again. But yeah, sure."

Zara leaned against the hood of their ride and winked. "Yeah, you're real fast, Damian, but not quite fast enough. Guess you'll have to just leave us alone now."

I fixed her with a look of steel. "That was the deal."

She shrugged innocently. "Yep. Fair's fair."

Irritation snaked its way back beneath my skin. Her father was like this. I narrowed my eyes and leaned in. "That was a hell of a gamble on your part."

"Not at all." She clapped her friend on the back. "I trust Rayne's driving more than anything in the world. Our ride, second. You didn't have a chance. Why, Rayne didn't ev—"

The she-devil snapped Zara gently with her tail.

Neve tugged on my arm. "Come on, let's get out of here."

I ducked back into the Rift and settled the ridiculous tab.

Zara was still inspecting the car when I came out. She mouthed *thanks* at me while her friend wasn't looking, and then turned back to her work, tinkering with something.

Obsessive. Precise. Talented.

Just like her father.

Regret pulled at me as we got back in the 'vette and drove away.

Neve

We turned off Razorback and cruised slowly up the Midway.

Damian looked drained, the normal fire in his eyes extinguished.

In the last twenty minutes, I'd seen fifty emotions cross his usually steely expression: protectiveness, frustration, excitement, irritation. I wasn't sure what they all meant. He was hard to read, which was, of course, why he was so good at lying. *To me.*

I had to remember that.

As I looked out at the buildings whizzing by on the right, Damian cleared his throat. "What did you learn from Zara? Why did I have to lose?"

He sounded a little peeved, and I forced back a smile. "Zara wanted to help. She couldn't talk while her friends were around. You were a diversion. Sorry."

A diversion. Something to shift everyone's eyes away while the real action happened in the background.

Just like the attack on the Archives. Perhaps like the prison curse.

The apple didn't fall far from the tree.

I wouldn't trust Zara for a second, except for the demon oath we took. I liked her, though, despite her penchant for snark. She believed in her friends. She wanted to help save the city.

Zara had given me a few more quick details about the realm Matthias was building, and I explained it all to Damian.

He whistled low. "He's making a world to use as a base of operations. We were always running, having to shift our forces, back when—"

He locked his jaw, and silence cut through the car.

The shadows in his eyes sent chills down my spine, so I diverted the conversation. "Matthias doesn't have everything he needs. He's missing an earth genie. And creating his realm is taking more power than he anticipated. He's draining magic from the ruins of a Magica city."

"Where's the city?"

"On the coast of the Black Sea. It's called Apollonia Parva, per Zara. I want to hit the Archives, see if I can find some maps or more information about it."

He tightened his grip on the wheel. "Well, this sounds like something we can use to undermine him eventually. But right now, we need to figure out how to stop the curse. My assumption is that Matthias is going to bide his time until the curse releases all of Bentham's criminals, and then he'll make his next move while we're distracted. Did Zara know anything about that?"

"Afraid not. But..." I rapped my fingers on the dash. "Maybe we can kill two birds with one stone."

"How so?" A spark of intrigue replaced the anger in his eyes. "To break the curse, we have to kill or banish the marid."

I nodded. "That means we have to lure it out. If we cut the power to his realm, Zara says that it will catastrophically destabilize the magic. I'm betting Matthias will send his genies to deal with it, or even come himself. We wait in ambush and hit them with a banishment spell as soon as they appear."

He frowned. "That's making a lot of assumptions."

My heart sank.

"But I love it." The car accelerated. "If it works, we banish the genies and break the curse. If Matthias doesn't bite, we still cut him deeply and cripple his operation. I like those odds."

"But then the curse..." I murmured.

Damian threw a hand in the air. "It's a gamble. But we have to outplay Matthias, and I guarantee he's already five steps ahead. We need to be unexpected. Plus, your precious Order should be trying to break the curse, too. If we fail, maybe they won't. This way, we're not putting all our eggs in one basket."

It was true.

Damian pushed the pedal further. "I'm tired of reacting. I'm tired of being surprised. It's time we go on the offensive and hit him where it hurts."

He turned, and his lips pulled up in a devastatingly sexy smile. "Your solution is brilliant, Neve. And he's never going to see it coming."

Warmth trickled across my skin until I glanced at the speedometer. "Uh, great. Thanks. But Damian, we're not racing now."

"The hell we aren't." He floored it, and we rocketed down the Midway, screaming by cars to the left and right.

We screeched to a halt outside the Hall of Inquiry.

Time to do my thing in the Archives—assuming they'd let me in after what had happened there today. My heart sank at the thought of all of those drenched books.

Damian was out of the Corvette in a flash and swung open my door. "I'm not coming in."

I gave a halfhearted laugh as I stepped out of the car. "I'm betting you're banned for life."

"Perfect. I can't think of a place I'd rather *not* be." He shut the car door and circled back to the driver's side. "If we're heading to the Black Sea, I have a lot of things to put in order. Call me when you know exactly where we're going."

His aura burned with confidence and energy as he slid into the driver's seat and sped off.

I headed toward the Hall of Inquiry. Security was tight. They'd erected concrete barriers and a new checkpoint...not that that would do much against a tsunami.

Or a hurricane.

I took the stairs two at a time and made my way to operations. Everyone was working around the clock, trying to find a way to break the curse. I gave Gretchen and Rhiannon the rundown.

Gretchen's eyes flashed yellow. "I like the plan. We can work things from this end. You'll need a banishment spell. I'll contact Ethan. He's already working one up for us."

"We'll also need some way to drain those magical batteries."

She nodded. "I'll ask about that, too."

Rhiannon slugged my shoulder. "That's great work, Neve. I'll come with you. I wouldn't mind having another chance at that djinn."

Gretchen shook her head and turned to Rhiannon. "Absolutely not. I need you here. I'm hoping you can look into the past and see how they cast the curse. It might give us clues about how to break it."

I tried to protest, but Gretchen's jaw was set.

Rhiannon caught my arm as I started to walk away. "Stay at my place tonight. We can have pizza. You can borrow some of my clothes and even your favorite pair of shoes."

Fates only knew when we were going to get out of here, but I thanked her with a hug and headed across the skybridge to the Archives. The building reeked of stale bilge water, and books were scattered across every available surface. Droves of imps flew about, hauling soaked volumes out of the stacks and casting spells to dry them.

This would take weeks to clean up. Chances were that many of the priceless books wouldn't even be salvageable. The part of me that loved the Archives deeply wanted to help—I could have turned myself into a human blow-dryer—but I had to focus on our mission: find the city of Apollonia Parva.

A low ache tugged at my heart as I headed back to the cartography collection. I was going to banish the heck out of this marid.

But nearly two hours of searching through the Archives revealed a single clear fact: every book, every map of Apollonia Parva had been stolen.

Matthias.

Had it happened during the attack on the Archives? Or before?

It didn't matter. Matthias had beaten us *again.*

Frustration wormed its way down to my fingers as I found another potential reference missing in the Special Collections. My fist flexed, looking for something to punch. Steam practically pouring out of my ears, I wound my way back to my desk and dropped into the chair.

Think.

Alexandria was off-limits, so the extensive library in Guild City was our best bet. But what were the chances that Matthias had hit their library, too? We hadn't realized anything was missing until I checked. My cell read eight-forty-five p.m. That meant it was nearly three a.m. London time. The library wouldn't be open for another six hours.

The curse on Bentham was just ticking away, and we'd already used up half a day.

I rested my elbows on the desk and ran my hands through my hair. The exhaustion of the day weighed me down, and my anger was the only thing keeping me going.

A moment later, Rhiannon's naturally chipper voice shook me from my daze. "I thought we'd find you here. Not going well, I assume?"

I leaned back. Ethan was with her. I was so drained I hadn't even noticed them approaching.

How had I missed his signature? The thundering hooves were almost deafening, and the rich aromas of hickory and earth permeated the air, practically drowning out Rhiannon's magic. He was definitely not suppressing anything.

Rhiannon was watching him with a familiar hunger

in her eyes. That didn't bode well—even I wasn't foolish enough to get tangled up with an archmage, no matter how charming. Then again, my type was apparently brooding FireSouls that lied about everything, so I had no room to judge.

I sighed and absently shoved some papers around on my desk. "We're screwed. Matthias, somehow, has stolen everything that ever mentioned Apollonia Parva. I'm going to try the library in Guild City when they open in six hours."

Rhiannon gritted her teeth. "Another point for the asshole. Lucky thing we've got some good news."

I rubbed my eyes and pulled my hair back. "I'm all ears."

Ethan laid a leather-bound tome on my desk. "I heard you like books."

I nodded, grabbing it eagerly. Magic surged through my veins, and I was suddenly very alert. This thing was oozing power.

"I inscribed the banishment spell into this spellbook. When you recite the incantation, it will blast the djinn and marid back to their respective planes. Forcing your will over them will take an enormous amount of power, so the other archmages and I pre-charged the spell. The thing is, you've got one shot, so make it count and try to get both at the same time."

"I assume, if I can only get one, I should try to hit the marid to break the curse."

"Precisely. Do you think you can manage the spell?"

I flipped through the pages until I reached a bookmark. The incantation was incredibly complex. I had near photographic memory, but this was going to take some practice. No way I could cast this without the extra power trapped in the spellbook. "I should be able to do this."

Ethan nodded. "I've heard rumors you're naturally talented with spellcasting. But you're not a sorceress. Or mage."

I shrugged and gave him a pointed stare. "Mages are always a little too interested in other people's business, for my tastes."

He winced. "Fair enough. We're curious types."

I would have loved to study as a mage. But then again, that would have entailed revealing I was half djinn to the very group of people known for casting spells to trap genies—so that was a hard pass. I sure as heck had never met a mage I trusted.

Anyway, I'd managed to figure it out well enough on my own.

I rose from my chair. "Thank you for the book."

"There's an incantation in the front. Read it aloud to bind the book to you. You'll be able to summon it from the ether. It's what I do with my collection."

I imagined how awesome it would be to have a library of spellbooks I could summon at any time. More than a little jealousy seeped into my veins. "Fantastic. I have a feeling that's going to be useful."

Rhiannon was practically brimming over with excitement and holding something behind her back.

I raised my eyebrows. "Okay, out with it. What do you have?"

"A jar of worms!" She whipped out a pint-sized glass jar filled with glowing blue goo and writhing black shapes and set it gingerly on the desk.

Ethan tapped it. "Be very careful with this. It's a sample of the devouring curse."

Horror filled me. "And you brought it in the Archives? Good gods, get that out of here!"

"It's a magic jar and almost impossible to break. If you press the gem in the lid with your palm for twenty heartbeats, it will bond to your magic, and you'll be able to summon it from the ether. Better than carrying it around in a backpack."

"All right, that's marginally safe. But why do I need it?" I bent down to examine the worm-like shapes as they wiggled about.

"This is plan B. If you can't figure out how to safely release the spells powering the batteries, then dump the curse on them. It will eat through and break the spells. As far as we can tell, the curse won't spread. At least in the case of the prison, it's very localized."

Rhiannon grinned. "We're turning their own magic against them."

"Heck, yes. I love it."

"Do be careful around the batteries. If they're old artifacts, the magic will probably be unstable. Dangerous." Ethan said.

I nodded. My friend Nix and her sisters had built a business recovering old artifacts with decaying spells, and I knew it was hazardous work.

I considered the little jar of destruction and Ethan's spellbook. This was good. I had a way to destroy the magic batteries and a spell to banish the genies when they showed up. Now all I had to do was figure out where the heck we needed to go. Hopefully, the library in Guild City would have some clues.

I stretched. I'd better let Damian in on the plan before it got too late.

Picking up the phone, I dialed his number, wishing Rhiannon were coming with us. I didn't trust him around me, or, more importantly, myself around him.

14

Damian

I clamped my jaw shut as Neve explained the situation. Matthias had outmaneuvered us again, and we were going to have to gamble he hadn't hit the library in Guild City. What a mess.

Flexing my fist, I calculated the time difference between Chicago and London. "Fine. We head to Guild City in six hours. Are you finished at the Archives? I'll pick you up in twenty," I said, then grabbed my keys and headed for the car.

"You're picking me up? What else do we need to do tonight?"

"You need to get some rest. Between saving the Archives and making deals with demons, it's been a long day. Since your apartment is gone, you can stay at my house. It's the safest place."

Silence cut across the phone line.

"No," she said at last. "I'm going to crash with Rhiannon."

Impatience pulled at me. "You're kidding. Matthias is probably hunting us. I wouldn't trust an Order safehouse, let alone your friend's couch. My place is secure."

"I'm sorry. I don't...feel entirely safe with you."

Her words cut deep, and heat flushed my neck. "I've had your back for the last two weeks, no questions asked."

"You lied about what you are," she said, practically under her breath. "I had to learn that by watching you rip the magic from the corpse of the efreet. I've asked you to be honest with me, but you've made it clear that I can't trust a word you say."

Anger seeped into my veins. "You lie to your bosses about what you are to protect yourself. I'm doing the same. The Order would hunt me down without question if they knew what I was, and you work for them."

Time stretched out as she didn't respond.

Damn it all.

"Fine," I capitulated. "If you don't entirely trust my hospitality, bring Rhiannon. I want you safe, and she can protect you, too. But my house is best. It's laced with enchantments, and I have security."

Neve sighed audibly over the line. "I'll talk to the Rhiannon and let you know what we decide."

She hung up.

My blood boiled, and flames flickered down my arms.

What the hell was that?

I strode to the Corvette, fired up the ignition, and then shut it off again with a curse.

Rhiannon was coming. The third wheel wouldn't fit in the 'vette.

My irritation was clearly clouding my thoughts.

I headed back in, grabbed the keys for the Porsche from Flint, and roared down the road. Halfway there, Neve finally texted: *Fine. Pick us up at the Hall.*

Be there in ten, I responded.

A few minutes later, I pulled up in front of the Hall of Inquiry. A new barricade and checkpoint blocked the entrance, and the watch had been tripled. Who were they thinking they were going to stop? Definitely not a genie.

I got out, leaned against the hood of the Porsche, and shot Neve a text: *Here.*

Minutes passed.

I glared at the bluecoats outside of the Hall. They exchanged nervous looks and seemed generally unsettled. Good. They should stay the hell back.

Finally, after about fifteen minutes, Neve and Rhiannon appeared in the massive columned entryway, backlit in soft sodium light. A man emerged with them, walking close to Neve. He was tall and muscled and looked like a fighter—the bastard who had healed Neve earlier. His aura was powerful enough to reach to the curb. Clearly, he was showing off. He touched her elbow in a familiar way, and she laughed at something he said.

Fire shot through my veins, and I started forward to intercept them. The last thing we needed was more Order operatives wrapped up in our affairs.

The man handed Neve a large book and an all-too-charming smile.

My fist wanted to crack his jaw.

A bluecoat moved to block my way, and several of his friends reached for sidearms. Hadn't they learned their lesson earlier?

Ridiculous security.

I stopped at the barrier. I didn't want to get Neve in trouble again.

My houseguests noticed I was waiting and headed down the stairs. Neve gave a friendly parting wave to the man.

"Who was that?" I said coldly as we walked back to the Porsche.

"Ethan, the archmage. You met him earlier." Neve slid into the passenger side as Rhiannon climbed into the back.

I swung around the front, got in, and slammed the

door. "I didn't know you were on a first-name basis with all of the archmages."

"Someone's in a foul mood."

I turned the ignition and revved the engine. "This place gets under my skin."

"For your information, Ethan helped me save the Archives today while you were poking around the citadel. He also gave us this." Neve held up the heavy book. "It's an enchanted spellbook, charged with power. It has a spell to banish the marid and the djinn. A banishment spell should work on them because they're not from this plane, in the same way it can work on demons. It won't on Matthias, though, since he's part human."

I ground my teeth as we rolled out. "Good to know. I'm glad you got it. Let's get the hell out of here."

The drive back to the breakers, on the north side of town, lasted an eternity. Neve made a pointed effort not to talk with me and chatted incessantly with Rhiannon the whole drive.

Message received.

I wanted a moment to talk to her, to smooth things over, but that wasn't going to happen with blondie glued to her hip.

That was fine. It gave me time to think. I wasn't sure what kind of trouble we were going to get into, but I was certain there would be some. Matthias would have his goons stalking us every step of the way.

I needed to do something about that.

I dialed the Apothecary, Alia. We had an arrangement, and she'd been equipping my agents with potions.

No answer.

It was late, of course, but she should pick up.

I tried again. Nothing.

Frustration tore at me. Was she screening my calls?

Not a great sign. A few days back, I'd sent the Alpha of the Guild City pack in her direction. Apparently, things hadn't gone smoothly, and Lachlan had wacked a number of her demon guards in the process of getting an audience.

Had she figured out who told him where she lived?

Alia might be holding me responsible for the mess, which didn't bode well for getting anything out of her tonight. Sorting things would take work and time we didn't have.

I swore after the phone rang to voicemail for a third time.

Neve broke off her chatter. "What?"

"I have a feeling that Matthias may put a tail on us. I haven't see one yet, but that doesn't mean they're not there. I was hoping that one of my contacts could supply us with a couple Potions of Seeing, but that won't be possible."

Neve pulled out her phone. "I've got a contact in the Shadow Guild who makes potions. She might be able to hook us up when we get to Guild City tomorrow. I'll text her now, but she's probably asleep."

"Excellent."

Neve returned to her conversation. Impressive. Even though she hadn't had access to her powers until recently, she'd built a wide network of connections. I wasn't particularly well-liked in Guild City, so hopefully, her contacts would come through.

The clock was ticking on the curse.

By the time we pulled into the driveway, my eardrums were exhausted from Neve and Rhiannon's chatter. Why hadn't I sent a cab?

The dark obscured the view of my massive yard, which ran down to the lakeshore. This type of property was nearly impossible to get in the city.

I parked, and we headed into the house. Chicago's city lights reflected on the water. I nodded to the two guards stationed out front and took the stairs two at a time. The last time Neve and Rhiannon were here, we'd had a fight, so I'm sure the place didn't bring to mind any happy memories.

I unlocked the front door and motioned for them to enter as my butler appeared in the foyer. "Flint. Show them their rooms in the south wing."

"Absolutely, Mr. Malek. I have already placed the clothes Jeanette picked out for Miss Cross in her room."

Neve raised an eyebrow.

Did she really think I would let her go trapsing around in Rhiannon's hand-me-downs?

Irrational frustration chipped away at me, and I headed for the kitchen. "I'll be in the kitchen making something to eat, if you're hungry."

I left before they could respond.

I wasn't going to call in Marcus, my chef, at this hour.

The refrigerator was randomly stocked. Clearly, Marcus had something planned, but I had no idea what it was. I grabbed an armful of ingredients and set to work.

Neve and Rhiannon wandered in about half an hour later.

Neve was wearing a new outfit—a subtly patterned blouse with a deep V-neckline and jeans. Jeanette had already mastered Neve's style, and I made a mental note to give her a substantial raise. She was absolutely invaluable.

The light blue hue of Neve's new blouse matched her skin perfectly, while the plunging neckline revealed a glimpse of the white tattoos that spiraled across her chest. Where did they wind to? Warmth flooded through me as my imagination took over.

Neve caught the direction of my gaze, and I snapped my eyes away.

The kitchen had a long island with seating. I never entertained in here, but I didn't cook often, either. I certainly wasn't trying to impress anyone. My guests had made it abundantly clear they didn't want to be here.

I set out plates. "Salad with fresh peaches. Bruschetta with prosciutto, ricotta, and cherries. It's light, but I didn't know if you'd be hungry."

"Thanks," Neve murmured. "I haven't eaten since breakfast."

"Chicago dogs," Rhiannon noted.

Fates. What a heinous choice for breakfast.

"Wine?" I held up a bottle of chilled rosé. They nodded, so I poured a couple of glasses and set the bottle on the stone countertop. "There's ice cream in the freezer. Flint is standing by. If you need anything, just ask."

Neve looked up sharply. "You're not joining us?"

Was that disappointment in her voice? After the barrage of mistrust?

I grabbed my phone off the counter. "I've got work to do. You should get some rest. We'll leave here at two-forty-five a.m., at the latest. We can grab breakfast in Guild City."

I started for the door, then paused. "I almost forgot." I snapped my hand out, and the new khanjar materialized in a ribbon of purple smoke. I set it down beside Neve.

"What's this?"

"You lost yours. I made it while you were gone. Hold it for ten minutes and concentrate on the blade, and it will imprint on you. After that, you'll be able to summon it from the ether. It's enchanted and will pack a little more punch than your old one."

She turned the curved blade over in her hand, tracing the wind-patterned pommel. "Thanks."

"It's nothing." With that, I strode out of the kitchen and through the back door. The night air was crisp. I circled the house, checking the magical wards and making sure my security team was in place. I'd made my fortune breaking into high-security zones, so I was the only one I trusted to set up the defense here.

Have I overlooked anything? The question gnawed at me.

I reached out and plucked one of the invisible wards. Its magic thrummed through my fingers, a subtle vibration like a spiderweb shuddering in the wind. The wards weren't strong enough to stop a genie for long, but they would give me time to get Neve and Rhiannon away. And they packed a few nasty surprises for the assailant.

The warm glow of the kitchen lights illuminated Neve and Rhiannon as they laughed, drinking wine. A hollowness formed in my heart, but I shoved it away.

I checked the positions of the snipers once again with my dragon sense and melted into the shadows.

I'd let Neve and Rhiannon enjoy the night while I worried about the darkness.

15

Neve

A blunt force shoved me. "Rise and shine! It's time to go get the bad guys."

"Nurrrrg," I protested.

"Come on, girl. Your phone alarm has been going off for, like, five minutes," Rhiannon said.

That explained the horrible buzzing.

I slapped my hand around on the bedside table. My phone was gone. I fished around under my pillow. *Bingo.* I snoozed the alarm and dropped the phone over the side of the bed.

"Neve, it's time to go."

"Ugh. It's comfy."

My tormentor pulled me out from under the covers. I sunk my claws into the pillowy mattress, but to no avail. "Just a few more minutes."

Rhiannon was already dressed and bright-eyed. She was always far too cheerful in the morning. It was deeply unnatural.

I sat up.

Where am I? This wasn't Rhiannon's apartment.

Reality hit me like a cold shower. Damian's house. We were heading to Guild City this morning. We had to break the prison curse.

Shit.

My heartbeat got up to speed with the situation as Rhiannon helped me throw myself together and marshaled me down the stairs. Damian was waiting and looking rather blurry. I rubbed my eyes. That was somewhat better.

"She needs coffee," Rhiannon said.

"I know, we've traveled together before. One for you, one for Neve, and I've got another for her for the road."

It was like listening to voices murmuring in a dream. Someone gave me a strong double espresso. It was dark and toasty and just slightly bitter. Perfect.

I drank the coffee as they ushered me out the front door and into an SUV.

Fates. It was still dark out. What an inhumane hour.

The ride was hazy. I knew I didn't drink *that* much

rosé last night, so this brain fog must have been the result of three hours of sleep and yesterday's tango with the water monster. Damian and Rhiannon were chatting about something, but I just watched the city lights speed by.

I checked my phone. Eve had texted me back. "Good news. My contact can bring us an assortment of potions. She says we can meet her at the Haunted Hound on our way into the city."

Damian nodded. "Excellent. We should be there in ten."

My phone pinged again. "Okay. She's wrapping something up but can be there in twenty."

A few minutes later, we rolled to a stop by the Circuit's central plaza. Tall glass buildings rose around us. It was still dark, and I couldn't see the lake.

"Next stop, London. Bring me back some HP sauce," Rhiannon said.

Right. She wasn't coming. I knew it, but my heart sank anyway, and fear crept into my gut. Was it really a good idea to be travelling with Damian alone? Shit. Probably—*definitely*—not. He was the most dangerous person I'd ever met. Worse, I tended to forget that fact when I was around him, lulled by his lies and rare but seductive smiles. His signature was like a drug: it made my head foggy and other parts of me very alert.

That kind of thinking was very dangerous.

I wished Rhia was coming along to help me keep my

head on straight, if for no other reason. But there was no point to wishing, at least in this case.

I gave Rhia a hug. "Crack the curse so we don't have to."

She grabbed my hand as I got out of the SUV. "Hey, now. I'm counting on you to banish those genies so I don't have to. I don't want to get captured and turned into a tea maid again."

I closed the door, and a pang of regret shot through me. I missed her already.

A gentle mist caressed my face as we crossed the central plaza. High overhead, an enormous water sculpture like a levitating river looped freely through the air —the Rain Bridge. It was lit with red, white, and blue lights at night. The monument was a partner to the silver Cloud Gate—also known as the "bean"—in Millennium Park downtown.

I finished the last of my espresso with a deep, contented sigh, and deposited the to-go cup in a nearby recycling bin.

Arched gateways ringed the plaza, which was one of the central hubs of the magical world. The portals were all oriented so that the first things visitors saw when they arrived in Magic Side were the rows of mirrored skyscrapers, Lake Michigan, and the Rain Bridge— symbolizing the union of magic, nature, and big business.

It was an unabashed PR move by the city.

Damian led us up to one of the Guild City portals. It was an ornate bronzework gateway with two glowing clock faces that read three-seventeen a.m. Chicago time and nine-seventeen a.m. London time. Damian adjusted a small dial until it read, *The Haunted Hound.* "After you," he said, and ushered me through.

I spun through the ether and stumbled out into a long hallway with shelves full of liquor bottles—not quite what I'd expected.

Damian emerged behind me. We headed down the hall and into a dimly lit pub decorated with old signs featuring unfamiliar beers. Patrons sat at dark wooden tables eating breakfast. The aromas of eggs and sausage wafted through the room, and my stomach grumbled.

Damian glanced toward my growling stomach, then quickly looked away. "We should probably grab something to eat while we wait for your contact."

Well, *that* was mortifying.

A man with golden-red hair greeted us. "Welcome to the Haunted Hound!"

Damian leaned over the bar. "Can we get a quick breakfast? Maybe tea for two and half a dozen fresh scones if you have them?"

"Sure, we can do that. Grab a seat."

We made our way to a table by the fire. Two ghostly dogs were snoozing nearby, probably the eponymous haunted hounds. It seemed like a wonderful place to be a dog. The slightest pang of jealousy shot through me as

I thought of the soft, warm bed I'd left behind. The fire warmed my skin, and I took a deep breath, trying to savor the moment.

I'd been running non-stop for a week—breaking into Helwan, escaping the efreet's tower, saving the Archives, and a dozen other adventures—and the clock was still ticking. If Rhia had been here, I would have begged her to stop time, just for a second, so that I could draw a single, unburdened breath. But she wasn't here, and I didn't have the gift.

A tall, slender woman approached. She had a blonde pixie haircut and gave Damian a broad smile. "Atticus isn't it? I remember you. I didn't think you'd actually drop by."

Atticus?

His eyes flicked guiltily to mine and then back to the woman. "That's right. Last time we met, you mentioned that I should stop in. Considering the circumstances of our encounter, I thought you might be able to help us out."

She raised an eyebrow. "Sure, what can I do for you?"

"I was wondering if you could point us to a potion shop. Maybe not one of the guild shops. An independent one that doesn't ask too many questions," Damian said.

"Ah," she said with a wink. "Absolutely. I know the

perfect place. I'll take you there myself once you've eaten."

I gave Damian a knowing look after the friendly woman wove her way back to the bar. "Atticus?"

"An alias."

Of course. Damian was a thousand lies draped in a cloak of deception. Hell, was "Damian Malek" even his real name or just another façade? Would he even know his real name anymore?

I twirled my hand, irritated and curious at the same time. "And what are these mysterious circumstances under which you met?"

Damian—or at least the man I knew as Damian— shot me a deadpan expression. "I was robbing a casino."

My fingers halted mid-twirl. I hadn't anticipated that one. "Really? And she was helping you?"

"No. I think she was helping to shake down the casino's owner. I didn't get the full story. We ran in opposite directions."

I laughed halfheartedly, unable to quite forget that this man never stopped wrapping himself in lies.

A few minutes later, the bartender dropped off a half-dozen orange-current scones with a side of clotted cream and jam. They were round and far fluffier than I'd anticipated, but they melted in my mouth. I wanted to savor them, but the clock was ticking.

Something in the fire looked at me, and I nearly jumped out of my seat. Spark hopped out of the flames in his dragon form and waddled across the floor.

The dogs made no movement at all. Distinctly not guard dogs, it seemed.

Spark sniffed one of the scones. *I wish to devour their essence.*

I slipped him one, hoping that no one would notice, as I didn't know bar etiquette rules here. Spark gobbled it down in three bites, and the scone turned to ash. *Mmmm. Fluffy.*

Partway through the plate of scones, a pink-haired woman drifted in. "Neve!" she said, smiling at me. "Good to see you so soon! And Damian? That's a surprise."

I stood and gave her hug. "You two know each other?"

She spoke with a charming Scottish lilt. "I met your handsome boxer just a few days back. I didn't expect to be seeing him again so soon!"

Boxer?

There was a lot I still didn't know about the man. Unsurprising, I supposed, for a criminal kingpin.

We took our seats as Damian cleared his throat politely, an uneasy expression on his face. "Glad to see you're doing well. Eve, is it?"

She pulled a bag from the ether, set it on her lap, and started rummaging. "That's right, I guess I didn't introduce myself the last time. I truly appreciate your help. We caught the man we were looking for."

Curiosity tore at me. Just how had they met? And how recently?

She smiled back at me and started setting potions on the table. "I owe you thanks, too! Hopefully, I can help both you two out with your problems. What do you need?"

A couple days back, I'd helped her break into the Archives. It was becoming a pattern with these Guild City folks. But favors for favors.

I sure wasn't going to admit to that in front of Damian.

"We're looking for a couple Potions of Seeing. We've had a few run-ins with invisible wind demons." I offered Eve a scone, but she shook her head.

She triumphantly held up a small blue bottle with gold flecks swirling in it. "I knew I had one! The potion will help you see invisible objects or creatures, but it only lasts about ten minutes. Afraid I only have one on hand."

"We'll take it," Damian said.

She pushed it toward him, then began stacking more and more potions on the table as she searched through her bag. "You definitely should take a healing potion. Those always come in hand. This is for invisibility. This is an acid bomb. This one will make you the size of an elephant—"

I placed my hand gently on hers to stop her from putting any more vials on the table. As a potion master, she was fine with all of this, but my heart was pounding. If someone bumped the table and these clattered to the ground, the mixed magical effects would wipe out half a city block.

She looked down at the pile. "That's quite a few I've pulled, isn't it?"

I laughed. "I'm not sure we'll be able to keep track of what's what... or transport them safely. How about we settle on the healing, invisibility, and potion of seeing?"

She smiled and began putting potions away. "Absolutely!"

Something ticked at the back of my mind. "We're going to be dealing with some powerful unstable magic. Old decaying magic batteries. Do you have anything to protect us against that?"

"Excellent thought," Damian whispered.

"Hmm, let's see. It's not a common request." She dug deep into her bag, then extracted a dusty vial filled with a black viscus goo. "Here! With decaying magics, you have to be worried about cellular damage, mutation, and, well, being blown to bits. I've got healing potions for cellular damage, and the protection against being blown to bits is your own common sense, but this should prevent mutation."

"Mutation...like cancer?" I asked.

"No. Mutation like growing tentacles and extra fingers."

I locked eyes with Damian. "We'll take everything you have."

16

Damian

Curiosity thrummed through me. Eve was certainly well supplied and clearly a master of potion craft. Why had she and Lachlan wanted to meet with the Apothecary? To discuss secrets of the trade? I hadn't asked at the time, of course, but now I was damned curious, especially since Alia wasn't calling me back.

I pushed a thick wad of bills across the table. "Thank you for your help. I expect this will cover it?"

It was always better to pay in cash, and I was ready to get out of here. I kept my various circles separate on purpose, and I didn't like the sudden convergence of acquaintances that was occurring in the Hound. Too messy.

Eve shook her head. "No. I owe Neve a favor. And really, you as well."

I took the potions and locked on her eyes. "You don't owe me any favors, as I've never done anything for you."

I really didn't want Alia knowing who sent them if she didn't already know.

She nodded, understanding the implication.

I shrugged. "Anyway, materials are expensive, and I like knowing the location of a well-stocked supplier. You can expect future business if you're interested."

She nodded and grudgingly took the money. "Really, I'm glad to help. Any time."

We shoved back our chairs and rose.

Neve gave her a quick hug. "We're headed to the library next. I've been before, but could you point us in the right direction?"

"Sure thing," Eve said, dismissing her bag.

I left some money on the table for the breakfast and followed them out as she reminded Neve of the route.

Urgency tugged at me as I followed Neve toward the library. I hoped this wouldn't take long.

That wasn't our only problem.

There weren't any signs of a tail, but the skin on the back of my neck tingled—the same feeling I'd had when we were infiltrating Helwan. Someone or something had started following us when we left the Hound. Either the Devil of Darkvale's spies keeping tabs on the city or, more to the point, some of Matthias's agents.

Neither boded well.

I fingered the Potion of Seeing in my pocket. If our tail were invisible, we'd have only one shot at taking them out. Best to wait a little longer and see if they revealed their intentions.

A few moments later, we came to a halt in front of a quaint Tudor building with dark timber framing, white plaster walls, and mullioned windows. "Is this the library?" I asked. It was rather small.

"Sure is." Neve knocked on the oaken door.

It opened after a few moments, and a woman with long, dark hair poked her head out. "Neve! I haven't seen you in an age! And who is your friend?"

Neve gave her a hug. "This is Damian. He's helping me with a case.

The librarian introduced herself as Seraphia and invited us in.

The interior of the library was extraordinary. A domed ceiling lit with stars soared overhead. Thousands of books stacked on polished wooden shelves lined the walls. The place was quite a bit bigger on the inside than out.

Joy palpably radiated off Neve as if she were a kid in a candy shop.

"I assume you've been here many times before?" I asked, leaning close.

"Twice," she said, almost in a whisper. "Long ago. It's more wonderful than I remembered."

The early morning light filtered down through the glass, catching thousands of dust motes dancing in the rays. Seraphia shut the door and swept over to us. "How can I help?"

"We're looking for information about the lost city of Apollonia Parva, and hopefully some maps," I replied. "We're working a case, but the person we're hunting stole all of the books on the city from the Archives."

Seraphia touched her hand to her chest. "I heard the Archives flooded yesterday, too. An absolute tragedy. I'm so sorry."

Neve wrote the name of the city on a slip of paper and handed it to Seraphia. The librarian motioned for us to stay in place and headed out into a tiled area in the center of the building. She waved her hands, and a massive bonfire burst to life. The green flames spiraled at least twenty feet in the air, sending a wave of heat through the building. Seraphia tossed the slip of paper Neve had given her into the fire, and a tendril of smoke snaked out of the flames and wound its way through the library.

I raised an eyebrow at Neve. "This is different."

"Instead of a computer catalog, they have a fire oracle," Neve whispered, as if speaking loudly would profane the space.

"Seems like an incredibly dangerous thing to put in a library."

A small flame erupted beside my shoulder as Spark

appeared in dragon form. He darted around the bonfire and back to us. *Dangerous? This is amazing—why aren't all libraries like this?*

"Paper," I suggested.

Seraphia pursued the thin trail of smoke deep into the library, and Neve absently traced her fingers along the shelves as we followed behind.

I hoped this was quick. It sure seemed like a slow way to find a book.

The whisp of smoke came to rest on a thick green book on a high shelf. Before Seraphia could grab one of the rolling ladders, Neve leapt into the air, snatched the book, and drifted back down, already leafing through the pages.

Neve frowned. "This is a nineteenth-century travel account. It says the city of Apollonia Parva was originally a Greek trading colony in the Black Sea, on an island near Sozopol, Bulgaria. The author hadn't visited it and includes only a few details. Is there anything else?"

Seraphia shook her head. "The smoke trail would have forked and pointed out any other relevant books. I wonder if its history has been scrubbed."

This didn't bode well. At least Matthias had missed one.

I drummed my fingers on the wood. "We're working with very thin information, here. I'd be a lot more comfortable about this if we had some clue as to what the batteries looked like."

Seraphia pulled out a wad of paper and a pen. "We'll just have to dig deeper."

We spent the next hour frantically poring through the library, searching for anything that might yield information tangentially related to Apollonia Parva.

Nothing.

The city had been scrubbed from the records, other than scattered mentions here and there in old history books. Nothing concrete. No maps or detailed descriptions.

My frustration finally peaked partway into the second hour. I rapped on the table beside Neve, who was buried in a musty old tome. "Okay, time's up. What do you have?"

She leaned back in her chair and shoved the book to the middle of the table. "Not much."

"Anything?"

"Apollonia Parva was a smaller satellite city of Apollonia Magna, which later became known as Sozopolis—the predecessor of the modern city. We'll just have to go there and find the island." She shrugged. "That's all I've got."

"Well, that will have to do. Time is slipping away. Anyway, this might be a good sign."

"How so?"

"One, Matthias doesn't want anyone knowing this

place exists, so it's important. Two, he clearly put a lot of effort into scrubbing the library and Archives, and he'll be confident in his work. He won't be expecting us to find it, so we might take him by surprise."

"I didn't think of you as a glass-half-full type," Neve said.

"More like the glass isn't entirely dry. Let's go."

Neve gave me a warm smile, which reminded me of the better times between us.

Seraphia came over and handed Neve a book. "This is *The Wanderer's Guide to the Magical Mysteries of the Balkans*. It doesn't mention your city, but it might have something useful. It's yours if it will help. Long-term checkout."

"Thanks, Seraphia." Neve opened the book and flipped several pages before tapping her fingers on a map. "There is a St. Ivan's Island right offshore of Sozopol. I've seen it mentioned elsewhere. I'm not sure, but it could be the place we're looking for—Apollonia Parva."

"So all we need now is a portal to Sozopol."

"That's something I think I *can* help with." Seraphia led us to an enormous open tome lying on a stand in one of the library alcoves. She started flipping the book's enormous pages over one at a time. "This book is an atlas of all the known portals. It looks like...yes, there is a portal in Sozopol, but the only access is from inside the Devil's tower."

Fantastic. That was going to be tricky.

Neve pulled out her cell. "I can call the Devil and see if we can get access. He owes me several favors."

Seraphia's eyes widened, and she excused herself as Neve made the call.

The Devil was a notorious vampire—perhaps even Vlad the Impaler—and the most powerful crime lord in Guild City. Curiosity gnawed at me. How did an Order operative like Neve get tangled up with a monster like that? I knew they'd worked together before—I'd even used that information to blackmail Neve at the outset of our relationship—but I still didn't know their connection. My muscles tensed at the idea of asking the Devil for help, but I let Neve do her thing.

A minute later, Neve hung up and grinned. "Okay, we can use the portal. The Devil gave me directions and a passcode."

"Good work. Let's go."

Neve pocketed her phone and gave Seraphia a hug. "Thanks so much for everything."

"Any time. Here's my info—that way, you won't have to make a special stop next time."

"Are you kidding? I'll be dying for an excuse to come back here. I could spend days."

I bid Seraphia a quick farewell and headed to the entrance. As soon as we stepped into the sunlight, my senses went on alert.

Someone was watching.

17

Neve

Damian's aura flared. He shifted his stance and lightly restrained my shoulder as his dark green eyes swept across the plaza. "We've definitely got a watcher."

I surreptitiously scanned the plaza before I started down the stairs. "I feel it, too. Try to act natural. See if we can spot them tailing us. Spark, keep an eye out."

The little dragon darted into the air. *Got it.*

Damian followed me through the crowded square. It was impossible to keep track of anyone here. We had to get out on a side road.

Spark zipped down as we turned onto a broad avenue. *I don't see anyone pursuing.*

"How much do you wanna bet we've got a couple of invisible wind demons trailing us?" I asked.

Damian flashed the small Potion of Seeing. "I thought we might ultimately have company. I was hoping the shop would have more. This will give one of us true sight for ten minutes."

I gnawed on my lip as a thought flickered to life. "Spark, can you drink a potion?"

I can consume its magical essence, so close enough.

"Remember on the airship, when you made the ice devils glow so we could see them in the storm? Could you do that to invisible creatures if you could see them?"

The little creature rubbed its claws together eagerly. *Yes. This is a delicious idea.*

"Let's lure them down an alley. Easier to target them and less collateral damage," Damian said, his voice low.

We pushed past cobblers and bookstores until I spotted a long, deserted alley and ducked left.

Damian followed and pulled the potion out of his jacket. "Showtime, Spark. Drink up."

The little glowing dragon darted forward and quaffed the potion. He belched a blue fireball, and his eyes started glowing. *That is vile magic.*

"What do you see?" I asked.

He looked around in a daze, as if completely stoned. *So many things. There are strange creatures like jellyfish floating through the air. And a nice ghost sweeping the streets.*

"Did it work, or is he high?" Damian asked.

"The wind demons. Are we being followed?" I pressed.

Spark spun into the air and quickly returned. *Yes! Four. They just slipped down the alley. They are staying far back. Watching.*

I stopped and pretended to read a pub menu hanging from a ratty looking door. "Okay, Spark, light 'em up. But don't let them know you've seen them. Maybe approach from behind."

Barbeque time. The dragon zipped off, and I lost him over the rooftops.

Forty seconds later, Spark dove out of the sky and flooded the alleyway with fire. As the magical flames died away, they revealed four wind demons, illuminated with glowing halos.

Spark zipped over our heads. *All yours!*

Damian pulled a bow from the ether and released three arrows in quick succession. One of the glowing demons exploded in a ball of crackling dark magic, but the other three shot into the air.

I soared skyward, looking for an advantage in altitude. One of the demons broke left and raced low over the buildings. I hammered him with percussive blasts of wind until he slammed into a rooftop, sending clay rooftiles scattering in all directions.

I dropped like a comet, but the wind demon flipped around and slammed a wall of wind into me. Gasping as the air was knocked from my lungs, I spiraled out of control and crashed into the roof one house over.

The demon spun as Spark engulfed him in a ball of fire. I sailed over the building and summoned my new khanjar from the ether. It materialized in a whisp of black smoke and thrummed in my hand, and as the demon spun, I drove the knife into its chest. Crackling magic surged through me and out the tip of the blade, spreading dark lightning though the demon's body. It exploded in a plume of dust, leaving a scent of ancient forests behind. A rush of euphoria washed over me.

This was Damian's magic infused into the blade.

Now, where was Damian?

I turned toward the sounds of battle in time to see one of the two remaining wind demons shoot a blast of wind into Damian's chest as he soared by. Damian went hurtling back against the gutter of a building and dropped to the street below.

I shot through the air, releasing a barrage of gusts at the demons.

Damian climbed to his feet, extended his hand, and shot a bolt of dark fire at one of the demons. Waves of flame coursed over its form. I slashed out with my khanjar, cutting through the fire into its back. It exploded and dissipated to nothingness.

The last wind demon shot skyward and vanished in a dusty whirlwind.

"Damn it!" I shouted. "He planes-walked!"

Damian flew up to meet me. "That's okay. He'll alert Matthias that we're on to him, but they don't necessarily know where we're headed."

"Then let's get to the Devil's tower and get the heck out of here before they come looking."

It took me a moment to get my bearings, but I soon had us back on track. The bustling crowds thinned out as we neared the Devil's tower. Drinking parlors that catered to dark tastes replaced the traditional quick stops and pubs. Finally, the streets opened into a green square. A savage black tower with red windows rose from the midst of the city wall and loomed over the open space.

We crossed to a large doorway flanked by a pair of bouncers dressed in black suits. One put his hand out, stopping our progress.

"We're expected," I said. "Nevaeh Cross."

He touched his earpiece and muttered something inaudible.

I flipped through *The Wanderer's Guide* while we waited for a response. The book was thin on facts, but it offered a little history, and it was instantly clear why the only portal was through the Devil's tower. The Bulgarian region of Sozopol and Burgas was rife with vampire legends. Apparently, vampirism had been such a problem in the Middle Ages that it was common for people to drive stakes through the hearts of people after they died.

Finally, the guards waved us through the doors. I could sense Damian's annoyance flickering.

The interior offered striking lighting and gleaming onyx black floors. While the modern décor contrasted with the medieval stone tower outside, both conveyed the same set of messages: power, wealth, danger.

A pale woman with dark hair swept down the hall to greet us. "Ms. Cross, Mr. Malek. I'm here to take you to the portal. Follow me."

We passed a cracked door that led to a nightclub, now deserted in the late London morning. She led us through a long corridor with numerous closed doors, and then down a spiral stair, deeper into the tower. At last, we came to a dusty room with niches inset into the stone walls. Many were marked with glowing runes.

The milky skinned woman pulled a black knife from her jacket, approached one of the niches, and slipped the blade into a thin slot in the wall. She turned the handle, and the runes above the doorway flickered out. "No one has used the portal to Sozopol in years, and we keep it locked. I'll lock it again behind you. You will not be able to return."

Damian nodded. "Understood. And thank you."

"Why is the portal locked?" I asked, not sure I wanted to know the answer.

"To keep our tower secure. And to keep the things on the other side out." She withdrew the blade and handed it to me. "Prick your finger and wipe your blood on the wall. The portal will suck you through. It's part of the magic. And don't worry, I don't mind the sight of blood."

Great.

I jabbed my finger and handed the blade to Damian. "Tell the Devil thanks. We owe him."

The woman smiled. "He knows."

As soon as I smeared my blood on the wall, the ether sucked me in.

18

Neve

The portal spit us out on an old, cobbled street. Brown wooden buildings rose around us, peaked with orange-tiled roofs that shaded us from the sun. The air was warmer than Guild City, and the squawking of seagulls drifted overhead.

I doubled over, fighting the wooziness that had taken root in my stomach on the roller coaster of a ride there. "Holy crap. Have you ever experienced a portal like that? That was almost as bad as planes-walking."

"Only once, in Tuscany. Ancient portals whose magic hasn't been maintained can sometimes bounce you around. Or fail to open. It was a risk," Damian said, looking as cool as a cucumber.

"Give a girl a heads-up next time, would ya?"

I glanced down the ancient street at a sliver of blue water glistening between the buildings. "The Black Sea. We might be able to see St. Ivan's Island from up there."

I'd never been to the Black Sea before, but I'd always been fascinated, especially now with the recent discoveries of perfectly preserved ghost ships. Boy, would Ronnie, my contact at the Field Museum, like to get his hands on one of those. He was *obsessed* with ancient shipwrecks.

My phone updated the time. Two-fifty-five p.m. We were eight hours ahead now, so it was probably an hour after dawn in Chicago. Way too early for all wind demons, vampires, and lost cities.

Maybe we could find some coffee here. I was running on fumes.

We walked several hundred feet, and the street sloped downward, revealing more of the topaz water. The houses were an interesting combination of stone and wood. Some looked several hundred years old, and potted plants decorated the upper balconies.

The sound of seagulls grew as we neared the waterfront, and a horde of tourists made their way down a stone quay, where half a dozen blue wooden boats bobbed in the water.

Sunlight cut across Damian's face as he stepped out of the shadows onto the promenade, highlighting his angelic features, both perfect and terrible. His signature thrummed around me and mixed with the sound of the gulls and the scent of the sea.

I could have gotten lost in the moment. Part of me wanted to hook my arm in his and stroll down to the shore, pretending I was on vacation in a quaint harbor town. That a timebomb wasn't ticking. That Damian was a decent man.

But he was a criminal, a liar, and FireSoul.

He wasn't able to conceal that part of his signature from me as well anymore. There was always the stain of the efreet's magic, reminding me of the dungeons and manacles and what Damian had done.

I stole my eyes from him, irritated with the butterflies in my stomach. I really had to get a better hold on my emotions. Remember who I was with.

"Is that St. Ivan's Island?" Damian asked.

The long, low island was at least a half mile away and looked pretty barren from where we stood. A few tourists clambered unsteadily into one of the boats, apparently heading over.

I pursed my lips. "Doesn't look like much."

"It doesn't *feel* like much, either."

Not good. But not necessarily bad.

"There's a chance the batteries' signatures are masked," I said, but Damian's silence wasn't reassuring. "Well, we'd better check it out to be sure. Looks like we can take a boat over." Of course, we could fly, but this wasn't a Magica city, and we couldn't risk being seen using magic. I started toward the stairs that led down to the quay, but Damian's hand grabbed my shoulder. "What?"

I caught the hardened expression on his face just as I felt their signatures. Well, their *lack* of signatures. It was the weirdest thing, like they were blank. The emptiness and silence they emanated was a dead giveaway.

Damian stepped in front of me. His magic flared, and heat rolled off him in waves.

Trying to ignore the way his magic made my brain foggy, I turned and counted five of them—four men and a woman—with the palest skin I'd ever seen, like snow.

"We don't want trouble," Damian said, his voice threatening.

His protectiveness was irritating. I could hold my own.

The man standing in front locked me with laser-focused eyes. "Interesting. What do we have here?"

He had what I assumed was a Bulgarian accent, and I was betting he was the leader of the bunch, judging by his arrogance. His jet-black hair was tied back in a pony-tail and made his skin look even paler.

"You used our portal but failed to pay the toll," the woman hissed.

Ponytail's lips curled up in a sinister smile. "What Elisabeta meant to say is your presence is requested."

Tension rippled in the air, and my eyes darted to the other vamps who had closed in around us. My hand glided to the hilt of my khanjar. The vibrations of its infused magic tickled my fingertips. I still hadn't gotten used to it.

"Not a chance." Damian's voice practically came out in a growl, and his muscles tensed.

Crap. Things were about to go tits up.

In a movement that was too fast to be human, the woman—Elisabeta—appeared beside me and grabbed the back of my neck, her nails digging into my skin. She probably would have torn my head off, but Damian had his hand around her neck in an instant. Anger coursed through my veins, and I felt the storm raging inside, desperate to be unleashed. "Get your hand off me, or you'll be sorry."

Damian tightened his grip around her neck. "You heard the lady. Release her, and maybe I won't rip your throat out."

Damian's magic felt dark, and I wouldn't put it past him.

Elisabeta's buddies arched forward in predatory stances, ready to attack.

"Enough." Ponytail raised his hand in a graceful motion. "Though we would be delighted to spill your blood, this is neither the time nor the place."

"Come on, Valko. Let me have her," Elisabeta said through clenched teeth.

Valko? So that was ponytail's name. It suited him.

He gave a commanding look to his companions, and

their bodies relaxed. "Elisabeta, come now. You know better. Kras would not be happy if you disfigured one of his guests. Especially one so beautiful."

I cringed as Valko's eyes took my measure like a creeper. Something about him made my stomach twist. Maybe it was the way the sun highlighted his veins beneath that papery white skin. What in the gods' names was he?

I still couldn't register their magic signatures.

Elisabeta's grip on my neck slacked, and her hand reluctantly retreated.

Valko sighed and picked his fingernails. "This can go one of two ways. Either you come with us for a chat or we turn this street into a bloodbath."

Damian released his grip and shoved Elisabeta back. She hissed, and two fangs shot out of her gums.

I took a step back, bumping into the metal railing. Okay, so that explained things.

Unlike the vampires in Magic Side and Guild City, these ones seemed shady as heck and maniacal. If it weren't for Valko here, I was pretty sure Elisabeta would have tried to rip my spine out.

Elisabeta's eyes shifted to me the way an animal locked on to its prey. She grinned, and blood flooded her irises. "I prefer a bloodbath. I could make a hat out of that one's ribcage."

Yup. Maniacal.

Valko chuckled. "Elisabeta has a tendency for *drama*.

Come, now, let us take a respite from this relentless sun."

Damian shot me a grim look and stepped behind as I followed Valko, no doubt shielding me from a sneak attack by the maniacs.

I glared at Elisabeta, and she showed me fang.

Rude.

19

Neve

The vampires led us down to the waterfront. Several passersby shot uneasy glances our way.

We turned and climbed a stone stairway leading to a two-story wooden house with a balcony overlooking the water, a dwelling larger than the others beside it. The idea of going with them to their lair made my stomach turn, but we couldn't risk a fight in broad daylight in a human city. The Order showed no mercy for those kinds of violations. The maniacs probably didn't care, but I didn't want to get locked up for the rest of my life. Or executed.

Damian strode confidently beside me, clearly irritated and ready to snap necks.

We could definitely handle a few vampires. Even weird ones. Probably.

Valko opened the antique front door, and we stepped inside. The air was cool and musty. I glanced around the dimly lit space at the strange decor—a vintage couch, a wardrobe with china, and an iron spike bolted to the wall.

These vamps sure had a strange style.

The floorboards above creaked, and I locked eyes with the figure who stared down at us from the second-floor railing. "My, my, Valko. What *have* we here?"

The man above, who I assumed was Kras, had a heavily accented voice. A patch of chest peeked out of the V in his shirt.

Valko crossed behind us and leaned in close. "They came through the portal but didn't pay the toll."

His warm breath itched my skin, and I bit back the urge to elbow him in the face.

"I see. Well, perhaps our visitors didn't know the rules that we keep here in Sozopol." The man above shot me a disconcerting smile.

"We didn't know of any toll," Damian said, his voice low. "But I assure you we can pay, whatever the cost."

"Whatever the cost?" The man flashed down the stairs at an inhuman speed and appeared before us.

I blinked twice. Okay, he was fast.

"We can talk cost later." The man swiped his hand through the air like this was an unimportant detail.

Then he turned and focused his dark brown eyes on me with a gaze that iced my skin. "First, tell me why you're here. We rarely have visitors. Not to mention ones so..." He looked to Damian and widened his eyes. "Unique."

"We came from Guild City," I said.

As soon as the words were formed, the man bared his fangs and hissed, still staring at Damian. "You're from Guild City."

Oh, crap. Wrong answer.

"Well, no. We're from Magic Side. Chicago?" I wasn't sure if these vampires had ever left Bulgaria.

The man's gaze darted back to me, and he smiled, the anger from seconds ago evaporated. "Chicago," he drawled. "And why have you come to Sozopol?"

"We're looking for the island of Apollonia Parva."

His eyebrows shot up as if I'd just said something remarkable. "Is that so? And what kind of business do you have on Apollonia Parva?"

I glanced at Damian, who looked more tightly strung than a violin. I was betting that he'd have slayed these vamps already if he didn't think we might get some information out of them first.

"There's a mage who's drawing the power from the batteries that conceal the ancient town. We need to disarm and release the magic so we can stop him." My voice came out stilted, even though I was trying my best to conceal my unease.

Damian tensed, and the corners of his mouth turned

down. He clearly didn't like me spilling the beans, but I wanted to see the vampires' reactions. There was a chance that they knew about the batteries and were even in league with Matthias. Better to know now than find out down the road, so I put our cards on the table.

The head vampire's face registered a little confusion, but he hid it quickly. He probably didn't know anything. The man bowed slightly. "I see. Well, then, welcome to our home. My name is Krasimir. This here is Valko." He gestured to Ponytail, and then to the woman. "And this is dearest Elisabeta."

He said her name affectionately, like she was a sweet little girl. I stared at Elisabeta, who was crouched on the couch. She cracked a lascivious grin at Krasimir that, with her untamed locks, reminded me of a wild animal.

I realized then that the other three vampires who'd cornered us in the street were gone.

"As it turns out, our goals may be aligned," Krasimir said with a hint of optimism, and then he frowned. "But where are my manners?" He strode over to a bookshelf lined with at least a hundred colorful antique books. Glancing over his shoulder at us with a flare of drama, he kicked the bottom of the shelf. "Like I said earlier, we don't get many visitors here in Sozopol."

The bookshelf slowly shifted and swung into the wall, revealing a dark wine cellar that extended at least fifteen feet.

Okay, so maybe these vamps have a sense of style, I thought, revising my earlier assessment.

"He means Magica visitors. We get a lot of Bulgarian tourists," Valko added.

"We're always open to new flavors." Elisabeta smiled, her eyes narrowing in on my jugular.

Krasimir reappeared from the cellar with a dusty bottle of what I was hoping was wine, though it was a little early to be drinking. The bottle had no label. He grabbed an ice pick from a drawer behind the bar in a blur of motion, then slammed the pick into the cork and ripped it out in one quick movement. He dropped the pick, still lodged in the cork, and poured four glasses that appeared on the bar top in a flash.

Krasimir crossed the room and handed Damian and me a glass. In another quick movement, he was in front of us, holding his own glass.

Now he was just showing off.

I glanced at Valko, who had also manifested his glass at some point, then down at the deep red wine in my cup. What were the chances that this was blood?

My eyes drifted up, and I caught Krasimir smiling. "It's wine. One of Bulgaria's finest, in fact. I have it bottled special for my reserve. Please."

I lowered my nose and sniffed the bold, fruity aroma. I was no wine connoisseur, but this smelled delicious. It tasted earthy and light, with hints of dried fruit and mulberry.

"You said our goals were aligned. What exactly is your goal?" Damian said.

Krasimir's mouth cracked up in a sly smile. "You're all about business."

My magic flared in my chest as I caught the way he was looking at Damian—the same way he'd looked at me earlier. Like a piece of cake, waiting to be tasted.

"Right," Krasimir said seriously. "Apollonia Parva is our home. Well, it was our ancestors' home for many generations until a wicked sorcerer cursed them."

"Wicked bitch," Elisabeta mused.

"Yes, well, the wicked bitch died, but the curse was never released. So long as her bones remain on the island, our kind are prevented from returning. And you see, while we love living in the Old City, we are just *dying* to get back."

This guy had flare. And I was beginning to admire it, even though he and his cronies still creeped the heck out of me.

"You can't retrieve the bones yourself?" I asked.

"Precisely. We cannot step foot on the island while the curse is in place. Come, now. Let us get some fresh air. It's much too dark and dank down here." Krasimir glided up the stairs, gesturing for us to follow.

Dark and dank, coming from a vampire?

I glanced at Damian. His expression was unreadable, but he'd unclenched his fists and seemed a little less tightly wound.

We climbed the wooden stairs and stepped into a room that opened onto a balcony. The breeze was refreshing, and I realized that I had a slight buzz from the wine.

Note to self—get a bottle to bring home for movie night with Rhia.

"Ahh, that's better." Krasimir closed his eyes and breathed in deeply. "Don't you *love* the way the breeze tickles your senses? Now, about our mutual interests."

He crossed to a wicker chair and took a seat. "You want to destroy the magic batteries on Apollonia. To do that, you need to find the island."

I gazed out at St. Ivan's Island just offshore. "Isn't that the island?"

Krasimir let out a hysterical chuckle, then cut it off short. "No, my dear. *That* is not. Apollonia Parva is hidden, and I guarantee that you will never find it without our help."

"Okay, so you want what? The bones of that wicked witch?" I asked.

"Wicked bitch," Elisabeta added.

"Precisely." Krasimir tapped his long, elegant fingers on the arm of the chair. His nails were perfectly manicured. "We'll take you to the island. You will fetch us the bones. And then you are free to do as you please with those batteries. Though I must confess, there is a high likelihood that you'll be blown to pieces if you try to release magic that unstable."

He had a point, and I still wasn't sure how Damian and I were going to pull it off.

"So, let's say we get you the bones. What then? Does the curse just disappear?" I asked.

Krasimir smiled. "Not exactly, but we have a sorcerer of our own. She will help us break the curse. Then, assuming you haven't blown Apollonia to Hades, we'll return."

"If we release the magic that powers the island's concealment, how will you deal with that?" Damian asked.

He was right. As soon as we drained the batteries, the island would be visible to humans. That would definitely raise a lot of questions.

Krasimir dismissed Damian's comment with a flick of his wrist. "Not a problem. We'll manage it. Do we have a deal?"

I looked to Damian, who nodded almost imperceptibly. I crossed to the balcony and watched the boats on the water, then turned to face Krasimir and his lackeys. "We have a deal. But you'll need to give us a precise location of the bones. And some supplies."

"What kind of supplies?"

My stomach growled. "Some food. A map of the island, if you have one. Oh, and a bottle of that wine."

Krasimir's lips pulled up in a sly grin, and he stood. "Deal."

The five of us returned downstairs, and Valko disappeared outside. Krasimir retrieved two bottles of wine from the cellar and set them down on the counter with a clank.

"Why is your portal sealed off to Guild City?" I asked. His earlier reaction to my mention of the place had piqued my curiosity.

Krasimir sucked his teeth, and his eyes flashed red.

"They say we're bad house guests." Elisabeta shrugged and leaned on the bar top.

Watching her closely, I could definitely see how that might check out.

Krasimir scoffed audibly. "They have so many rules over there. You can't do *this*, you must do *that*. It's a bore. Plus, if you ask me, those Guild City vampires are savages." He leaned forward and emphasized those last words, and I nearly choked.

As far as I was concerned, every vampire I'd ever met seemed like an angel compared to Krasimir and his lair mates. Is that what they were called?

"What does a vampire do for a living these days in a place like Sozopol?" Damian glanced at the selection of books on the shelf, and his eyes fell to the strange iron stake on the wall.

"We eat tourists." Elisabeta drifted around the bar, her movement graceful like a predator. Her eyes homed in on Damian, blood pooling in them as she watched him. My magic wound tightly in my chest.

"True." Krasimir grinned. "But that's not *all* we do."

He crossed over to an antique writing desk and fetched two brochures from a drawer. In an instant, he was standing in front of me, a little too close.

I glanced down at the brochures that he'd slipped in my hand before reappearing at the bar in a streak of movement.

I'd never get used to that.

Vampire Tours of Old Sozopol.

I nearly choked out another laugh but stopped myself. "Are you serious?"

Krasimir tilted his head. "We do what we must to get by. Tourists love vampires, and we love tourists. Our guides show the highlights of the Old City, and sometimes, they add a little flavor."

Elisabeta laughed, and I caught the drift. "Speaking of which, Kras," she said, "these two still haven't paid the blood toll for their passage through our portal."

Krasimir looked at Damian and me with a pensive stare. "You're right, Elisa. What are we without our traditions?"

I wasn't liking where this was going. I took a step to close the distance with Damian. If we were going to have a fight, better to keep our flanks guarded.

Seeming to sense my unease, Krasimir beamed. "Oh, not to worry. We don't follow our traditions exactly as our forefathers did. This will be painless, I promise." He pulled a small knife from his pocket and glided toward us. "I just need a drop from each of you."

I rubbed my fingers together and realized that the cut from earlier had healed. *Damian.*

"Just a drop." Damian raised his palm to Krasimir.

Krasimir jabbed Damian's index finger and pulled out a white handkerchief from his pocket, holding it below Damian's hand. Bright red blood pooled, and a drop stained the fabric before his skin sealed shut.

"Excellent. And now you." Krasimir turned to me, and I extended a finger. Elisabeta had inched closer and was watching me with those blood-red eyes.

He pricked my finger and took a drop of my blood, then placed the handkerchief to his face and breathed in deeply. "Most excellent. Your blood toll has been accepted."

"Somehow, I was expecting worse," I whispered to Damian as Krasimir turned away.

Krasimir's head snapped back, and he smiled broadly. "It's always nice to do a tasting. You sample our wine, we sample yours. Such exotic flavors. So much potential. Truly unique."

He tossed the handkerchief to Elisabeta, who took a quick sniff. "Definitely drinkable now, I'd say, though I suppose it could stand a little more time in the barrel."

Krasimir shrugged. "Now that that's done, are you ready to fulfill your end of the bargain?"

I took a breath to ease my rising nerves and gave Elisabeta a sidelong glance. "Sure. Let's go find the wicked witch."

20

Damian

We departed Krasimir's house and headed down the stairs toward the sea. I kept a close eye on Elisabeta. The way she kept watching Neve made me want to snap her neck.

Krasimir seemed reasonable enough, but I still didn't trust them. Vampires that went off on their own were unpredictable, and unlike Guild City, there was no authority in Sozopol to keep them in check.

"As per our deal, here is a map of Apollonia Parva." Krasimir handed Neve a yellowed roll of parchment secured with a red ribbon. "It's a historic map and won't have nearly as many details as Google, but it should serve your purposes."

Neve untied the ribbon as we made our way to the waterfront. Valko and Elisabeta walked ahead, discussing something in low voices. They turned down a set of stairs leading to a dock, where a small fishing boat was unloading its catch. Otherwise, the rocky anchorage was empty.

"This will be great. Thank you, Krasimir." Neve had partially unrolled the parchment, and I caught a glimpse of the outlines of an ink drawing.

An agitated voice drifted up from the dock as the three of us neared the stairs. Below, Elisabeta had a fistful of the fisherman's shirt. Her hair blocked my view of her face, but his was red and angry, and when she leaned in close, fear flashed across his eyes.

I started down the stairs, my patience with these vampires waning.

"What's going on?" Neve said, no doubt referring to the commotion on the dock.

Krasimir smiled broadly. "Oh, nothing to worry about. Elisa and Valko are just procuring our transportation."

Krasimir probably wouldn't kill a man in broad daylight, but Elisabeta was a lunatic, and I wouldn't put anything past her. I crossed the narrow dock, stopping behind Elisabeta. "Let him go. I'm sure we can make an arrangement with this man that will be worth his while."

Elisabeta's head jerked back at me, her eyes hungry

and fangs ready. "Keep your mouth shut. This is the way we do things around here."

My dark angel rose, and magic coiled in my fingertips, heat rippling down my arm.

Valko stepped forward and placed a hand on Elisabeta's balled fist. "Calm down, Elisa. Let's not put off our guests."

Elisabeta released her grip with a sneer. Valko leaned in close to the fisherman, locking him with a hypnotic stare. The man's shoulders relaxed, and his eyes stared blankly at Valko.

I shook my head and glanced back at Neve. She stood on the dock, clutching the map, her eyebrows pinched together. Her hair was radiant in the late afternoon sun, and I had to pull my eyes away from her.

"That should do the trick," Valko said enthusiastically. "All aboard."

The fisherman stumbled past me, his eyes glassy, apparently in a trance of some kind. He was lucky to leave with his life.

Elisabeta jumped in the small trawler and was at the helm in half a second. Valko followed. He stooped and picked up a few flopping fish with a look of disgust painted on his porcelain face.

I stepped into the boat and turned, extending my hand to Neve. She paused on the dock, then took it and stepped down, her hair brushing my shoulder as she passed by. Her scent wrapped around me for an instant, running over my nerve endings before the breeze carried it away.

The rumble of the engine and the stink of diesel cleared my mind. I took a seat at the bow near Neve. Krasimir appeared beside her on the wooden bench, flashing me a knowing smile. I bit back my emotions and stared at him coldly.

The boat pulled away from the dock, and as soon as the water turned a darker shade of blue, Elisabeta throttled the engine. We pulled out of the rocky anchorage and veered right, heading south along the coast with a trail of whitewater in our wake.

Neve unrolled the map in her lap, her focus drawn to the black outlines of the island and the various scribbles of writing. I made out several handwritten notes beside the original Latin descriptions.

"This is where the mausoleum should be located." Krasimir tapped his finger on a rectangular structure on the northern tip of the island. "Of course, I've never seen it on the ground. But this is what's on the map, and we've scouted the area from the sea several times. This is where you must go. I assume the batteries are located in the south, near the main ruins of the city and the Temple of Apollo."

"Okay. So first, we'll retrieve the bones. Do we have to worry about any traps or spells?" Neve leaned forward, scooped up a fish, and absently tossed it over the side of the boat, her eyes never leaving the map.

"Perhaps," Krasimir said. "Be prepared for anything. Though I imagine the curse on the island would have been enough of a deterrent. I shouldn't expect there to be any threat to you."

Unlikely. The mausoleum would most certainly be guarded. The question was, by what?

We rumbled down the coast, passing little clusters of houses perched along the shoreline. Their orange roof tiles cut a striking contrast against the rocky landscape.

I glanced at Neve, absorbed in her map. Flames pooled in my chest. I was getting accustomed to my new magic, and the sensation was oddly pleasing.

"Does anybody live on the island now?" Neve asked.

"No. Not since late antiquity. When Rome fell, trade routes in the Black Sea changed, and Apollonia Parva declined. After a few centuries, the remaining inhabitants left. That is why it is in ruins."

Sunlight danced across the glassy blue water. Apart from a lone fishing boat in the distance, there was nothing out there. Suddenly, my fingertips went numb. I glanced at Neve, who began rubbing hers together. Apparently, she felt it, too.

Nausea hit next, like a sledgehammer. It was like we had just passed through a wall of sickly magic.

In the distance, the outlines of a rocky island appeared. The nausea grew.

Neve placed her hand on the gunwale and closed her eyes. "Fates. Is that the island's signature?"

"Yes. Lovely, isn't it?" Krasimir chirped. "Each year, I swear it gets worse."

I reached into my backpack and found the tiny vial of anti-mutation potion we had purchased from Eve. She hadn't indicated precisely how long the potion would last, but it was probably best if we could hold off a little longer. I also didn't want to use it in front of the vampires.

Valko tossed me something from the stern. I caught it and glanced down at the yellow wrapper.

"Suck on this. It helps ease the stomach," he said, then tossed one each to Neve and Krasimir.

I bit down on the yellow candy. Its tart citrus flavor soothed some of the nausea.

The wind had picked up, and the boat bounced over the crests of the waves. Neve leaned forward, shielding the map from a burst of sea spray. The sun kept creeping across the sky. It would be dusk in a matter of hours.

Fates be damned.

This side trip was going to cost us time. Luckily, we still had around twenty-four hours before Bentham fell. *Probably.* The sooner we banished the marid and djinn, the better. The sooner I could best Matthias...

Flames licked down my arms, barely visible in the light. Nobody had seen them...except, of course, Neve. Her frosty gaze all but extinguished them.

Elisabeta shut off the engine, and the boat slowed, gently bouncing in the waves. "This is as far as we go."

"Yes. You two will have to swim the rest of the way. I am afraid we cannot risk getting any closer," Krasimir said.

"Do you know what would happen if you got too close?" Neve broke her gaze from mine and rolled up the map.

"Ohhh. I do sometimes wonder." Krasimir gave Neve a broad smile that summoned the dragon within me.

Flames cascaded down my arms again, but I snuffed them out. I cleared my throat. "Once we retrieve the bones, how will we get them to you?"

Krasimir cracked a grin and locked me with crazed eyes. "We will be waiting outside of the island's magic field. Bring them to the beach. We will see you and return. And do make haste." He tilted his head back and squinted at the sun, which hung low in the sky. "We'd rather not spend the night on this boat."

Valko handed Neve a fistful of candies, which she stowed, along with the map and supplies that Krasimir had given her, in the backpack. I slung the bag over my shoulder and met her gaze. "Ready?"

She rose and waved at Krasimir. "We'll be back in a jiffy."

He cocked his head and frowned.

Neve launched into the air, causing the boat to lurch. The three vampires watched her, and then their heads snapped to me, a glimmer of surprise etched across their hardened features. I stepped onto the bench, released my wings, and jumped into the air.

The vampires crouched low as the wind from my ascent pummeled them. As I rose into the sky, I heard Krasimir's voice from below: "Well, I'll be damned."

21

Neve

The warm air rushed past me as I soared into the bright sky. Despite the sickly sensation of the corrupted magic in my gut, elation filled me. I slowed and turned, catching sight of Damian heading my way. He was glorious. His dark wings cut a striking contrast with the fiery sky. Below, the vampires stood in the boat watching us, mouths agape.

I laughed. "Probably weren't expecting that, were you, Kras?"

I dove and crossed Damian's path, taking in the extent of Apollonia Parva. It was bigger than I'd expected, and I was glad the island's magic didn't prevent us from flight. After spending my life grounded, I'd never take flying for granted.

The faint outlines of the ruined city and the Temple of Apollo rose from the waves at the far end of the island. A shiver of fear crept over my skin as the weight of what was in store pressed down on me.

Could we do what was necessary?

Damian appeared at my side, and I pushed the worry from my mind. First, we had to retrieve the witch's bones for Kras.

I had a feeling this wasn't going to be as easy as grabbing a milkshake at DQ.

I turned my gaze north, listening to the sound of the fading motor as the vampires sped away toward the outskirts of the island's magic field. They probably hated the feel of the magic as much as we did and didn't want to be anywhere near the cursed grave.

The mausoleum was perched on the farthest tip of the island. Its white stones looked dull in the fading sun, and the overgrown grasses that surrounded it swayed in the wind. We were looking at the back of the structure—its front must face the rocky shore that was pocketed with tide pools.

I landed on the remnants of a stone-lined pathway that appeared to have once bordered the mausoleum. The ruins of ancient structures filled the landscape, their foundations peeking up through the undulating grasses and wildflowers.

Damian alighted near me. He retracted his wings and inspected the surroundings, his jaw set.

"What's wrong?" I popped another hard candy in my mouth, thankful Valko had given me a couple of extras.

Damian's eyes tracked my movement, and then he reached into his backpack. "Something's wrong here. The magic is off."

He pulled out the tiny vial of potion that we'd picked up from Eve and popped the cork with his thumb. "Drink some of this."

"Are you sure we shouldn't wait?" I would give just about anything to rid myself of the sickly feeling of this place, but I didn't want to burn through the potion. The unstable magic around the batteries would be exponentially worse as we closed in on them.

"Just take a sip. There will be enough." He pushed the vial toward me, and my fingers brushed his, igniting a flurry of feelings in my stomach.

Mind over matter, Neve. Apparently, my libido was having none of that.

I shot back a sip of the potion and grimaced as the bitter liquid burned my tongue. At least it cleared my head. The nausea lifted immediately, and I breathed in a sigh of relief—from the nausea *and* the questionable thoughts. "Thank you, Eve."

I handed the vial to Damian, but he didn't take any, just slipped it into the backpack.

"Aren't you going to take a sip?"

He glanced at me and started toward the mausoleum. "I'll be fine. I want to make sure we have enough for later."

Wasn't that what I said?

I glared at him and followed. His righteous chivalry was pissing me off. "Hey, you don't have to—"

He paused and raised his arm, motioning me to stop. "Do you feel that?"

I acquiesced, despite my irritation. Energy zinged through the air, faint and subtle but definitely there. "Now that you mention it, yes."

"Like I said, the magic here feels off. It could just be the island."

Shivers raced down my arms. "Or it could be something else."

Damian shot me a look that did nothing to calm my unease. "Let's be quick about this. Stay alert."

He didn't need to tell me. My senses were on overdrive, ready for boogeymen to jump out of the grass at any second.

I gripped my khanjar as we skirted the rectangular mausoleum, the magic from its blade instilling me with a surge of confidence. Damian had infused the blade with his magic when he forged it, and his aura vibrated through me. I tasted salt and smelled the deep scent of forest and smoke. Holding the khanjar was almost like touching him. Warmth flooded though me as I briefly thought of what that would be like...

I forced the haze from my mind, concentrating on the signature that he had stolen from the efreet, reminding myself of the danger from him and from the island around us. There was a timebomb ticking. A deadly island. A witch's curse.

Losing focus now could mean losing everything.

A set of double stairs fronted the building, leading to a single arched entrance. Damian took the left, and I crept up the right. We flanked the open doorway and peered inside.

Empty.

It was comprised of a single room. A section of the roof had collapsed, and the waning light of the sun cast a faint glow on the back corner of the space.

"Here goes nothing," I breathed, stepping into the mausoleum. Broken roof tiles and stones littered the floor. A frieze of faded frescoes decorated the walls, depicting all sorts of plants and animals—peacocks, wolves, dolphins, and a strange two-headed sea creature. It was exquisite, and a deep sense of awe filled me as I realized that we were probably the first people to gaze upon these walls in centuries, if not a millennium.

"A hydra," Damian murmured.

The hair on my neck stood on end as I followed his gaze to the fresco on the wall. One of the most famous creatures from Greek mythology. I leaned forward and inspected the snake-like creature, trying to recall what the myths had said about it. "I thought the hydra had a dozen heads." This one only had two.

Damian turned away and stepped over the scattered debris so he could inspect the frescos on the far wall. "It varies, depending on the myth. But yes, hydras can have a dozen heads. They regrow if they're cut off, or so the myths say. Unfortunately, there's usually some truth in them."

Damian lifted a massive slab of stone from a pile of debris at the back wall and tossed it to the side like a sack of potato chips. "Look at this."

I broke my gaze from the hydra on the wall, and my breath caught. Damian stood over a small stone sarcophagus. I was so enthralled by the frescoes that I hadn't had a chance to inspect the rest of the room.

I dismissed my khanjar and carefully stepped over the tiles and stones, making my way over to him as excitement tickled my skin. Damian crouched next to the sarcophagus, his hands tracing the cracks in the stone. It was about the size of a medium cooler chest.

"I don't sense any magic seals." He looked up at me, and my breath stilled. His eyes glowed with the thrill of discovery, making him seem almost human.

Gods, when he looked at me like that, I saw a softer side to him that twisted my heart. Was I mad to think of him as anything but a killer? A thief of magic?

As much as I fought it, I knew he was something more.

Damian slid the lid of the sarcophagus off and rested it against the back wall. I leaned over to find a small box inside. It was made of wooden panels that were crudely nailed together. The rough box exuded a sharp magical signature that tasted like wine and seawater and smelled of dried herbs. It sounded like cracking rocks and felt like the cold night air.

"Whatever is in there is pretty powerful," I said. "Do you think it's safe?"

"Probably not. But I don't detect any traps." Damian reached down and pulled it out, resting it on the corner of the sarcophagus. He brushed off the dust that had somehow accumulated on it, revealing a gap between two panels.

I kneeled next to Damian, ignoring how the heat from his magic twined with mine, and peered through the gap between the wooden panels. He clicked on a flashlight that he'd manifested from somewhere. The contents of the box were bundled in a tattered, cream-colored cloth. I tilted the box to get a better view, and excitement flared when the ball of what looked like a humerus shifted out from under the desiccated fragments of cloth. "Bingo."

I glanced over at him. Flames pooled in his eyes, and he watched me closely with a look that sent tingles up my thighs.

Oh, gods.

I stood abruptly and dusted my hands on my pants. "Well, this has to be it. We'd better get a move on."

Traces of a grin flickered on Damian's lips, and he returned the lid to its place. "Yes. We'd better." He picked up the box and slung it under his arm, and my eye caught something on the front.

"Wait. What's that?" I took the box and wiped the panel with my forearm. Sure enough, there was painted black writing on the front—Latin, by the looks of it.

Damian frowned and cocked his head as he read it. *"Behold, Zephyrus blowing from the north."*

Shocked, I stared at him blankly. "Since when do you read Latin?"

Another mystery to add to the pile.

He looked up and shrugged. "I've had a lot of time to learn. It's very rusty. There's more: *The seed of Typhon and Echidna rises forth from the depths. Death will swiftly follow."*

My skin prickled.

"Are you sure you read that right?" I squinted at the inscription. My Latin wasn't remotely serviceable.

"Yes, I'm sure."

"So, is it a curse?"

"Don't know. That seems like it should be Krasimir's problem. We've got enough curses on our hands. Let's just not open it." Damian took the box from me, concern in his voice.

"Yup. Great idea." I turned and headed toward the

door, then noticed that the waves outside were crashing onto the shore. "Oh, crap."

The sea had been calm a few minutes ago.

I stepped out onto the stone landing above the steps. The wind whipped through my hair, and a gust pushed me back. Damian appeared at my side, his shoulders taut.

"Zephyrus," he whispered.

I looked at the raging sea, and fear iced me. "Um, Damian. Who is the seed of Typhon and Echidna?"

Damian set the box down, then summoned a smoking blade from the ether. He turned to me, flames flickering in his dark eyes. "Hydra."

Fates.

The inscription wasn't a curse.

It was a spell.

And just by reading it, Damian had cast it.

22

Damian

I gripped my blade and scanned the roiling sea.

Hydra.

I'd heard the myths many, many years ago. A serpent with heads that regenerated, and blood that was poison.

I turned to Neve. Her hair whipped in a wild mass around her, and the urge to protect her shot through me. "Take the box to Krasimir."

Her head snapped in my direction. "And leave you to deal with the hydra? No way."

She held her khanjar, determination written all over her face. There'd be no changing her mind, I knew that. But I didn't like it. "Fine. But keep a safe distance from it."

She nodded and launched into the air. Neve could take care of herself better than most people I knew, but worry still sickened my thoughts.

I tucked the box inside the doorway to the mausoleum and returned to the landing, unleashing my wings. Waiting for the water beast to show its faces.

As if reading my thoughts, a dark shadow appeared offshore, and two heads erupted from the churning sea. Their eyes blazed with an unearthly light. Water cascaded down their long necks, their skin black and glassy like oil.

Flames rose across my skin as I flexed my fire magic. The faint stirrings of the dark angel rumbled, but I locked it down. The powers within me competed for my energy. They seethed beneath the surface of my skin, eager to break free, calling for me to use them. Ice. Fire. Dark magic. Amidst the cacophony of voices, the only one I could hear clearly was the one that craved for more—FireSoul.

I leapt off the stairs, and my wings caught me and carried me over the gale. Pulling my bow from the ether, I unleashed two arrows in quick succession. One flew wide, while the other narrowly missed one of the hydra's heads.

The beast whipped around and lashed out with unbelievable speed. I dodged, but the monster's black neck slammed into me, and pain shot through my back. I spun downward, pulling out of the tumble right before

I hit the water. The hydra snapped at me, but I soared out of its reach.

I resummoned my bow and fired two more arrows, which struck home. The hydra's body quaked as the dark magic in the arrows worked its way into the beast's flesh. It released a high-pitched roar, deafening and shrill, like a train screeching to a stop on iron rails.

Neve soared over the hydra, blasting it with gusts of wind from behind. It lumbered forward through the waves, raging and distracted.

This was my shot.

I summoned my blade and dove, aiming for the nearest neck. "Let's see if the myths are true," I muttered.

At the last second, the hydra's cunning eyes snapped in my direction, and its head shot toward me like a cobra. I spiraled out of the way as its jaws snapped the air beside me, raining bile and stinging spittle across my skin. Before it could strike again, I whirled around and sliced through its neck with three savage blows.

The monster reared up and roared as its severed head dropped into the water. But before I could take another breath, two ghastly plumes of flesh and smoke spiraled up from the stump, forming two new heads.

The myths were true. *Great.*

Neve swooped down beside me and unleashed a roaring vortex of wind. The monster staggered back, pinned against the rocky shore, and she screamed above the wind. "I'll hold it down! Spark says we have to cauterize the wound with fire!"

The little dragon whipped through the air beside me, belching forth a stream of fire, as if to make the point.

With no time to lose, I dove for the newly formed heads, fighting against the force of the wind. I summoned the efreet's magic, and flames burst from my blade. Dodging the creature's serpentine strike, I slashed through the growing necks with two swift strokes and cauterized the gaping wounds. The hydra bellowed in rage, making my ears ring and vision blur... but the heads didn't reform. Fire was the key.

And now there was only one head left.

The wind around me picked up as Neve intensified the storm, directing a waterspout straight into the creature. It shrieked and fought for balance as the sea around it churned and whipped into the air. She was glorious to behold, wind tearing at her clothes and hair, magic crackling around her like lighting. She met my gaze with glowing eyes and nodded.

Then something shifted below the sea. Before I could cry out a warning, the hydra's tail flicked out of the water several hundred feet behind Neve and crashed into her, sending her flying into the brush along the shore.

I flew forward as fast as I could.

Neve clambered to her feet and summoned her khanjar, while Spark whirled around her.

What the hell was she doing?

The monster's massive, spiked tail smashed down beside her and snapped along the ground. It slammed into her, catapulting her body into the shallows.

I pushed forward, my wings straining against the wind.

Neve staggered up out of the water, her tattoo burning with red light.

No time.

My wings burst into flame, and the efreet's magic pushed me faster than I'd ever flown before.

I grabbed Neve and pulled her to my chest just before the monster's tail rammed into the shallows, showering us with rock and debris. My wing clipped a bush, my bones cracked on impact, and we hit the ground hard. Agonizing pain dimmed my vision, but I broke our fall with my body, and we rolled down the embankment along the shore.

I released her and surged to my feet, retracting my broken wings with a tortuous crunch. "Fly! Pin it down!"

Shock streaked across Neve's face, but she launched into the air as the hydra thundered up out of the sea toward us, quaking the rocky shore. Chest heaving, I summoned my sword and sent the efreet's fire rippling along the blade.

As the hydra's savage jaws snapped forward, I leapt

to the side and swung my blade into its neck with all of my strength. Metal hit flesh, but at the wrong angle, and the blade didn't cut all the way through.

The creature bellowed and swept my feet out from under me with its spiked tail. I rolled onto my back and summoned my shield, bracing myself as the hydra's jaws bore down. Two fangs pierced the shield and buried themselves in my left arm, splintering bone and sending blinding pain coursing up my limb.

The monster shook its head and flung me into the air. I crashed into the shallows and felt bones in my arm snap. The pain mixed with the sickly fire in my veins.

Poison.

As I staggered to my feet and drew my blade, I called for the efreet's fire.

But no magic came.

23

Neve

My heart started beating again as Damian rose from the water.

I called a whirlwind down from the sky, pinning the hydra.

I'd been trying to channel Spark's fire magic when Damian had knocked me out of the way. Now the fool man was going to get himself killed.

Spark spiraled around me in a state of panic. *You must summon my fire through our bond.*

I gritted my teeth as I poured my strength into the whirlwind. "We tried that. The hydra almost got us."

Damian ran across the rocky shore. Even though it

was restrained, the hydra lashed out. Damian dodged, seemingly sluggish, almost drunk.

Crap. This didn't bode well.

Using all the magic I could summon, I pushed the creature's head back, trying to give Damian an opening. He swung his blade against its neck, blow after blow. Blood poured over him. Suddenly, the hydra's roars were silenced as its neck snapped free and crashed to the ground.

Then Damian collapsed, motionless.

Spark flapped anxiously beside me. *I think he is dying.*

I darted down as fast as I could fly. "He's not dying. He can heal himself."

I shouted his name, but he didn't move. Something was wrong.

Smoke swirled up from the hydra's neck as two new heads formed.

Oh, shit. Why hadn't he used fire?

Spark's voice rang in my head. *You must complete our bond. Summon my flame.*

Panic spiked, but I pushed my doubts away and reached for Spark's magic.

My tattoos flickered with orange light, but nothing came.

Desperation tore at me, and I summoned my khanjar. Its power vibrated through my body, giving me strength. I had to do this. I focused my mind on Spark, on the bond that had united us across the planes.

And I called his fire.

Searing flames burst from my tattoo and wove around my hand. They snaked across my fingers and disappeared into the hilt of my khanjar. A sheet of fire erupted from my blade as the warmth of Spark's magic flowed through my body.

Now we're cooking.

The hydra had retreated, waiting in the tide pools until its heads regrew. They were about the size of papayas, their little necks no wider than my arm.

I shot out low over the water, careful not to alert the hydra to my presence. The wind whipped across the sea from the north, and I had to steady myself with magic. As I got close, one of the hydra's heads turned back, locking on me with those beady eyes.

The creature's tail snapped out of the water, but I was ready for it this time. I darted sideways, dodging the attack, and flew straight for the head that had spotted me.

And I was fast.

The heads snapped at me like twin vipers, but I moved like the wind and sliced through both sprouting necks in a single clean stroke. Flames erupted from the blade, and the severed necks sizzled with fire. The hydra writhed in the water, trying to douse the flames, but they would not be quenched. The fire glowed blue, and the hydra's inky flesh began to dissolve into a plume of smoke. In seconds, the body disappeared into mist, and the wind stopped.

It was as if the monster had never even existed. I pulled the khanjar close to my chest and smiled as I felt Spark's fire magic pouring through me.

Amazing.

Seeing Damian's crumpled body, however, extinguished any excitement that I had about this new bond with Spark. I raced back to the shore and dropped to my knees beside him, ignoring the bite of the sharp rocks. Why hadn't he healed? Fear raced through me. "Damian!" His eyes were closed, his skin clammy. "Wake up." I nudged his chest, but he didn't move. "Where's your backpack?"

We'd purchased a healing potion from Eve. If Damian's magic was somehow blocked, that would surely work, wouldn't it?

Please, gods, let it work.

I scanned the embankment but didn't see the bag. Damian cracked open his eyes. "Mausoleum. Beside the box."

His voice was strained, and every muscle in his body had tensed. He must have been in serious pain.

My heart pounded in my ears, and adrenaline coursed through me. If I could just get Eve's healing potion, Damian would be fine. I jumped into the air and was on the landing of the mausoleum in seconds. Grabbing both the backpack and the box, I returned to Damian.

I reached into the bag, my fingers fumbling among the bottles. Glancing at the labels, I recognized the green healing serum and uncorked it. "Damian, you have to drink this." I gripped his jaw with trembling fingers, and he opened his eyes, his pupils dilated. I lowered the vial to his lips and tilted it so the liquid poured into his mouth. His throat clenched as he swallowed the healing elixir. Anxiety tore at me as I waited, but seconds later, color returned to his skin.

"Thank fates," I sighed, slumping to the ground. The heaviness in my chest lifted. I corked the bottle and stored it in the bag, then glanced at Damian.

He opened his eyes and raised himself on one arm. The potion seemed to be working.

That was a close call.

I glanced at the pink sky as the sun hung low above the horizon. "Crap." I stood and picked up the box of the witch's bones, clutching them to my side. "I'll fly these over to Krasimir before the sun sets. You stay here and heal. I'll be right back."

Damian stared at me with intense eyes that I couldn't read. "Fine."

He wasn't fully recovered yet, and that worried me. But I needed to get these bones to Kras, and then maybe we could find a safe place to recuperate. According to my calculations we had until tomorrow night to drain the batteries. I launched into the air, climbing high above the island.

I glanced down at my khanjar. It no longer glowed, and I felt no heat from it. Worry filled me.

Was Spark okay? I hadn't seen him reform after he melded with the blade.

I decided to worry about that later. Spark often disappeared. I guessed it had something to do with regenerating his magic, which could only be done in the Realm of Fire. At least, that's what he'd told me after our battle with the efreet.

The rocky shoreline of the mainland was etched with crags and gullies in the fading light. The water was glassy, and a light breeze blew from the west. I searched for Krasimir's boat.

There.

The white and red fishing boat was up ahead, a mile out. My magic surged, and I pulled myself through the air more quickly. Though they were specks from this height, I was pretty sure Valko was waving at me.

I angled downward and slowed myself as I approached the boat.

All three vampires were on their feet. Valko was beaming, Elisabeta frowning, and Krasimiar was...well, he looked paler than normal, if that was even possible. He was clearly in shock.

I hovered beside the boat and handed the box to

Krasimir. He clutched it to his chest and looked down at it, as if he didn't believe it was real. Turning his gaze up to me, he smiled broadly. "You actually did it."

"We had lost hope and were about to leave," Elisabeta said dryly.

"Pshh. We did not. We knew you'd pull it off." Valko winked at me, still beaming.

"Well, that had better be what you're looking for, because we had a hell of a fight getting it," I said.

Krasimir flexed his eyes. "Oh, really? What was it? A chimera?"

"A hydra."

"Ohh. Deadly. I hope you didn't get bitten."

Fear iced me. "No, but Damian did. He's okay, though. We had a healing potion."

"I see." Krasimir knit his brows thoughtfully, and then he smiled. "Well, then, we've both fulfilled our ends of the deal. It was nice doing business with you. Do stop by when you've finished here."

Elisabeta passed Valko a wad of bills. Had they been betting on us? *Those bastards.*

She started the boat's engine, and it screamed to life. "Good luck!" Valko called, and waved to me as they pulled away, heading north toward the coast.

There better not be a chimera on this freaking island.

I turned and flew back to Apollonia Parva. My thoughts turned to the hydra, and frustration welled in my chest.

Why had Damian been so stupid? Stepping in front of the hydra and getting bitten—what the heck was he thinking? He'd risked everything back there. I couldn't release the power from the magic batteries alone. And if we failed, the wards on Bentham would fall. Magic Side would be screwed.

By the time I closed in on the island, I was fuming. But I also realized that something else was bothering me, and it had nothing to do with the curse on Bentham or Matthias and his genies.

It was something that had been revealing itself over these past weeks that we had worked together.

I cared for Damian.

Fates. *Now* who was stupid?

I *hated* Damian. He'd lied to me, and he might literally be the death of me. Not to mention he had a way of sparking my rage.

I flew faster, trying to clear my thoughts. I'd hoped this flight would cool my anger. Instead, I was ready to throw down on Damian. After all, I had important questions that needed answering. Why had he given me the khanjar? Why had he been so reckless, risking himself with the hydra?

I landed on the rocky shore in front of the mausoleum, ready to tear Damian a new one. But he was gone.

My pulse quickened, and I glided along the coast,

searching for him. Dread squeezed my chest like a vice. Had the hydra returned and snatched him?

He was nowhere to be found. I rose higher, scanning the tide pools, then the area around the mausoleum.

Movement caught my eye, and I relaxed as I recognized Damian. He'd made a small fire on a sheltered beach in the lee of the island. I flew toward him, my anger only heightened. Was my anger rational?

Definitely.

Damian crossed the beach into the water as I landed by the campfire. He either hadn't noticed or was ignoring me. That final thought added fuel to my internal blaze.

The water lapped at Damian's thighs, its calm surface still reflecting the final hues of sunset. In a swift movement, he pulled his long-sleeved shirt over his head and dropped it in the water. Streaks covered his broad shoulders where his wounds had healed.

My anger from earlier mixed with the heat that pooled in my belly—no doubt a combustible combination.

He released his wings, and my breath caught. They were at least six feet across, and the black feathers on their bottoms dipped into the water.

I watched as he washed the blood from his arms. Memories of him almost dying flashed in my mind.

My skin chilled.

Why did I care? He was dangerous. Deadly. More importantly, we could never be together.

And yet, he was all I could think about.

Shrouded in the dying light of the day, Damian was an angel of darkness, magnificent and terrifying.

And I wanted him.

24

Damian

I released my wings, and with them came a modicum of relief and control.

While Neve was bringing the witch's bones to Krasimir, I'd managed to rein in the dark angel. But it still called out to me, beckoning to be freed.

The problem was, the more I embraced my dark magic, the more I was tempted by my desires. I'd learned the bitter truth of that many years ago. The line between light and darkness was thin, and once I'd had a taste of the dark, I knew which side I'd likely end up on.

Blood dripped off my body, mixing with the seawater before dispersing. Even with Eve's potion, I felt the hydra's poison working its way through my system. My wounds had finally healed, but I was fatigued.

I'd sensed Neve's return. She was on the beach, her aura blazing like a sun.

I almost hadn't been able to protect her.

My muscles tightened, and I splashed water on my face, hoping it would douse my pent-up anger and frustration. What had she been thinking? Risking herself like that—for me.

I looked up at the fiery sky where the sun had dipped below the water. Darkness was closing in.

My thoughts kept returning to Neve, and anger coursed through me. Anger at her impetuousness. At her insistence on doing good, even if it hurt her. But mainly, anger at the way I'd felt when I'd seen the hydra barreling toward her.

I scrubbed my face. Get a hold of yourself, man.

"You shouldn't have pulled that reckless stunt back there, Damian. It was stupid." Neve's voice cut through the air like a bowstring.

Heat streaked through me.

"I had it covered," she snapped, and I could tell she was out for blood.

Flames licked down my arms, and I turned. "Had it covered?"

Neve stood in the lapping waves, the usual softness of her body now rigid, her anger palpable. Her red hair wrapped around her shoulders, and in the dying light, she was radiant.

Gods be damned.

"You almost died, Neve. And you would have, had I not pulled that stunt." Thunder churned in my chest, and I cut through the water toward her.

"I could say the same about you." Her eyes flashed with frustration. Fear.

I towered over her, taut with tension. Her jasmine scent wrapped around me, flowery and heady, rousing something within.

Where had these feelings come from?

The dark angel stirred, taunting me to give in to my deepest desires. I needed to put some distance between us to get a hold of myself. "I need a minute."

My voice was like gravel. I turned and strode toward the rocky promontory at the end of the beach.

"We're not done here, Damian." Neve charged after me. "Why did you risk your life for me?"

Why indeed? I'd never risked myself for anyone before.

Heat rippled off me, turning the water droplets on my skin to vapor. "It was nothing. Split-second decision."

"*Nothing?* It wasn't nothing, you idiot."

I spun, tension pulling at every muscle in my body. "What do you want me to say, Neve? That I care about you? That I want you?"

I was playing with fire.

"I—" Neve's voice faltered, color rising in her cheeks.

"Of *course* I do." The words burst out of me before I could stop them. "But you've made it clear how you feel. And hell, maybe you're right. Maybe we're a bad fit. We're dangerous together, that's for sure."

Neve stepped forward, her chest rising and falling. "I don't know what I want anymore."

"Well, be careful, because I know what I want." I gripped her arms, and her energy coursed through my fingers, adding fuel to the inferno of desire rising within me.

Neve's eyes locked on to mine, burning with intensity. Fury. Passion. Twisting her arm from my grip, she slid her hand to the back of my neck and yanked me toward her. The length of her body pressed into me as her mouth crushed into mine.

An aching groan escaped me, and no longer able to resist, I scooped her into my arms, kissing her with an urgency that threatened to rip me in two. She wrapped her legs around me, her thighs clenching tight.

"Damian," Neve whispered, breaking her lips from mine. "I want *you*."

Whatever restraint I had was gone. I clutched the back of her head and dragged my lips down her neck, grazing her collar bone with my teeth. She trembled under my touch.

"Yes," she whispered, and her legs clutched me

tighter. Heat poured through me, and I tensed with desire.

I carried her to the beach and lowered her onto the sand. She grabbed the bottom of her shirt and dragged it over her head, then dropped it beside her. Her skin was soft and flushed. My lips found hers, and I drank her in, running my hand down her quivering side and flicking open the button to her pants.

I leaned back, taking in the sight of her sprawled out before me, wanting. I clutched her waistband and lifted her hips, pulling her pants off in a quick movement and tossing them away. Planting my hands on either side of her, I lowered my face to her neck, tasting the salt on her skin. "Is this what you want?"

"Yes." She pulled me onto her, wrapping her legs around me. Her warm skin pressing against mine was almost too much to bear. Pleasure and pain tore through me as her lips and tongue swept across mine. She kissed me desperately, and I slipped a hand under her ass, pulling her heat into me, needing to feel and taste every inch of her. She moaned, and her hand slipped between us, reaching for my jeans. Her fingers grazed my skin as they searched for the button, sending arcs of electricity through me.

I tore my mouth from hers and grabbed her wrist softly. "Let me take care of you."

Desire cascaded through me, and my voice came out deep and rough. I lowered my face to her chest, breathing in the sultry mix of jasmine, citrus, and heat. My lips followed the delicate outline of her breasts that peeked out of her black lace bra. As I tracked my mouth down her stomach, her body trembled, her chest rising and falling as she panted for air.

My fingers traced the silky fabric of her panties, feeling her tantalizing heat. "Gods, I want you," I choked out. "May I?"

"Yes." Her voice was breathless and full of need, making me want her even more.

I slipped them off, desire and pleasure and tightness inundating me. I grazed her inner thigh, slowly working my way to the magic between her legs. When my lips found it, pure bliss shot through me, plus the overwhelming desire to be inside of her. Her body quivered, and a low moan of pleasure escaped her lips.

Fighting back the yearning that racked me, I followed every whimper, every movement she made, until she was on the brink.

"Damian, please." Breathless, she tried to pull me up on top of her. "I want all of you."

I gazed up at her, sprawled out before me, a feast for the eyes. Her magic poured over me, and I wanted to drink it in. Taste *all* of her.

A tightness clenched my chest, and I reached my hand and placed it on her stomach, pushing her down. "No. I can't."

I gripped the base of her thigh and kissed her center.

Heat and tension coiled tight, and my need to be inside of her was almost too much. My stiffness ached as her skin quivered beneath me, her magic vibrating the air and humming in my ears like a siren's song. She dropped her head back, and her body arched as I brought her over the edge, her magic exploding around us, sending arcs of energy across my skin.

Pain, desire, and craving overpowered me. Gods, I wanted her, in more ways than one. She stirred feelings and needs I hadn't sensed before. She was intoxicating, and I felt my control dissolving.

No.

How had I given in to my desires so quickly? I was a fool to think I could control myself. Every second I was close to her, it frayed further.

Fear pierced my heart.

When Neve reached for my hand, I pulled back from her and rose.

"Damian, what's wrong?" She sat up, clutching her shirt to her chest.

"This was a mistake."

"Why?"

"Because I'm a FireSoul and fallen angel, and I'm losing control. I can't be close to you. Not anymore."

"What does that mean?" Pain flashed through her eyes, another lance to my heart.

"It means I'm dangerous. That I'm no good for you. Once this job is over, we should part ways."

"Don't you think I can make my own decisions?"

Her voice was sharp, but I could see the truth in her eyes. She knew this was dangerous, that *I* was dangerous.

I turned and left.

Neve

Embarrassment and hurt hit me like a rogue wave as I watched Damian scoop up his shirt and walk away.

Heart pounding, I stared out across the bay. The sky was darkening, and the water gently lapped against the sand.

Fates, how had I lost control like that? How could one of the most amazing experiences I'd ever had also be one of the most stupid and humiliating?

Shaking my head, I shook out my sandy clothes and dressed.

By the time I'd finished, a rising tide of frustration had washed over me. Why should *I* feel bad about what had happened? He was the one who'd kissed me back, did those *amazing* things, and then just stormed off like a lunatic.

Shivers raced down my thighs at the memory of his

touch, but then pain exploded in my chest when I recalled his cold words. Did he really want to part ways?

Being with him was insane. Impossible. Why did my body feel this way about someone I clearly couldn't be with?

He'd spelled it out—his desire for my power might kill me. And even if that weren't the case, how could I be with a crime boss from Chicago's Underworld and still take my job seriously?

Kicking up sand, I crossed the beach to the campfire and grabbed Damian's backpack. I snatched the bottle of wine and corkscrew Kras had given us out of the pocket and slumped down near the fire.

Damian had disappeared, and it was better that way. I couldn't face him right now. My nerves were too raw.

I pulled out the cork and took a sip of the wine. What I needed right now was Rhiannon and Amira. Girls' night on the beach, roasting s'mores in the fire. My stomach grumbled, and I reached into the bag and pulled out the biscuits and salami Valko had packed.

Not s'mores, but they'd do in a pinch.

I took another swig from the bottle and watched the stars peeping out from the heavens.

My mind wandered to Spark. I was relieved he hadn't been around for *that* fiasco. Gods, that would have been embarrassing for a number of reasons.

I sighed. We had a big day ahead of us tomorrow. I

needed to clear my mind. And most importantly, I needed rest.

What had happened with Damian had been great. But he was right—he was dangerous, and we were a bad fit. It would be better if we didn't go down this rabbit hole. Plus, I didn't want a guy like him, anyway. There was good in him, but too much bad. Too much danger.

Truth be told, my life was better without him.

Exhaustion crept over me, and I curled up next to the fire, using Damian's backpack as a pillow.

I watched the flames of the campfire dance over the twisted branches and fell into a deep sleep.

25

Neve

I woke as the sky was lightening.

Almost dawn.

I yawned and sat up, noticing the jacket that was draped over my shoulders. Not mine.

Turning, I caught sight of Damian kneeling across from the dying fire. His eyes met mine, and my pulse quickened.

I thought we decided we were done with this, Neve.

Damian's jaw was rigid, his expression unreadable. He stood and walked toward the sea.

I stretched and climbed to my feet, feeling refreshed and slightly more clear-headed than the night before. At least my embarrassment and frustration were gone.

There was definitely something between Damian and me, but I couldn't let it go any further than it had. Damian was an asset, that was all. We had to focus on breaking the curse on Bentham and banishing the marid.

I summoned the spellbook Ethan had given me from the ether, then focused on memorizing the spell as I munched on a PowerBar. While I had a near-photographic memory for text, I had to understand the intricacies of the spell. The incantation was convoluted and would take much longer to cast than I would have liked. Of course, we were trying to banish a genie from this world—it wasn't going to be a walk in the park.

Damian returned after half an hour. I quickly dismissed the spellbook and blushed as if I'd been caught doing something illicit.

"Ready to fly?" he asked. Though he'd cooled off from last night, he still seemed wrought with tension.

"Yup. Let's figure out where we're going."

I pulled out Kras's map and spread it on the ground between us. The temple of Apollo was at the southern tip of the island, about two miles away.

Damian tapped on the map. "I should be able to pinpoint the exact locations of the batteries once we we are close. Let's go."

Heck, *I* could probably detect them. They were oozing magic, and the sickly feeling was churning my stomach.

I folded the map and tucked it in the back of my jeans. Damian gave me a nod, and we leapt into the sky.

We flew south in silence as the sun rose out of the sea, casting fiery orange-pink streaks across the sky. The ancient ruins of Apollonia Parva whizzed by beneath us, shrouded in overgrown vegetation. Up ahead, the crumbling walls of a ruin rose out of the water—the temple of Apollo. Several other buildings dotted the rocky shore around it. We slowed and landed on a spit overlooking the partially submerged temple.

The air vibrated, and nausea washed over me— worse than it had yesterday when we'd entered the island's magic field. "The batteries are close. And definitely unstable."

Damian set his backpack on the rocks and handed me the anti-mutation potion. I took the vial and swallowed a gulp. The relief was instantaneous, and I felt even more refreshed than I had the first time.

I handed the potion back to Damian, and he took a sip. Judging from the contents in the bottle, there'd still be enough if we needed another dose.

He turned to me. "There are two batteries. I can sense their signature, one more strongly than the other. Both are underwater."

Underwater. *Of course.*

The fates were really messing with me lately.

I pulled the map out of my jeans and stored it in

Damian's backpack. "I don't know about you, but *I'm* ready for an early morning swim."

He watched me closely as I peeled my jacket off and tossed it on a rock. I swore I saw flames flicker in his eyes, just like last night when he kissed me and—

Desire pooled in my belly. *Oh, fates.*

His eyes bored into me, the flames in them growing.

I quickly summoned the jar of worms from the ether. "This is the sample of the devouring curse I told you about."

He carefully took it from me and peered at the writhing black things in the neon blue liquid.

Nothing takes the heat out of a moment like a jar of worms.

"These are the same as the curse infecting Bentham?" He turned the jar over in his hands and gave it back. "And we just release them and hope they're drawn to the batteries' magic instead of ours?"

"That's what Ethan said."

Damian scowled. "That doesn't up my confidence."

I sighed and dismissed the jar. "We need to discuss what happens after we cut off the batteries."

He nodded. This was the tricky bit. "We don't know how long it will take for the worms to eat through the spells, nor do we know how long it will take before Matthias and his genies notice their power sources are weakening. Just in case they respond quickly, we should release the worms and hurry back to shore as quickly as possible once we know the plan is working."

I pointed to some ruins a few hundred feet from the shore. "We can hide there. We'll be able to see the temple with enough standing cover to avoid detection. I'm hoping the horrible, corrupted magic around here will mask our signatures."

"How long do you need to cast the banishment spell?" Damian asked.

"Less than a minute."

Concern etched its way across Damian's face. That was a horrendously long time in combat. "Hopefully, they'll be focused on the batteries, and they won't notice you casting until it's too late. And remember, the marid is the priority. Banish him, we banish the curse. If both genies show up, focus on him."

I nodded, a pit forming in my stomach. Now that we were here, this plan seemed crazy, and I looked at Damian as fear tugged at me. "No heroics this time. I can handle myself."

He shook his head. "That's a two-way street. If things go wrong, planes-walk out immediately. I can do the same. We'll meet up in Magic Side at my house."

I gave a halfhearted smile. "Okay. Let's do this."

I followed Damian to the shore, and we dropped our bag in a corner of a colonnaded courtyard right at the edge of the sea. Further out, toppled limestone columns broke the surface of the water. The corrupted batteries were close, bleeding unstable magic into the air. I swallowed the bile forming in my throat. The sooner we were out of here, the better.

"Here we go." I stepped over a chunk of limestone and found my footing on the bottom. The water was chillier than I'd expected for summer.

Damian led the way, and soon, we were waist-deep in the water. The southernmost tip of the peninsula must have sunk at some point, and much of the temple's architecture was fully submerged. Seismic activity?

A fish brushed against my calf, and I jumped. Damian looked back at me, his face blank.

I shrugged. "Don't act surprised. You know I hate water."

Looking down, I could make out the faint outlines of my legs and the bottom. At least it wasn't dark water. I'd take all the small mercies the fates would give me.

After a few more steps, I was treading water. Damian was taller than me, so he still appeared to be standing on solid ground. I cast an air bubble over my face and ducked under.

Broken lintels and columns scattered the bottom below us. I turned and made out the rectangular foundation of the temple stretching for several dozen feet. Although the marble was covered with algae, the temple was remarkably well preserved. In an alternate universe, I'd have been an archaeologist. There way too many magical ruins just waiting to be explored.

As I scanned the bottom, I caught sight of Damian diving down to a pair of collapsed columns. I hadn't cast a magic bubble over his face, so he was holding his breath.

I darted toward him using a small push of magic. Controlling it was becoming second nature now, and I'd almost taken it for granted. Almost.

The water around us vibrated with magic, giving it a strange, almost oily quality. Though the sea was clear, it was difficult for me to see. Nausea squirmed in my stomach, and I had to work hard to keep my breakfast down as I was gently nudged by the currents.

I pulled up beside Damian as he lifted a column and dropped it to the side. Even underwater, that must have weighed a half ton. Literally.

The water was icier here, and as the sediment settled, the outlines of an ornate piece of limestone appeared. It was carved with scrolls and vegetal designs, and I quickly recognized it as the base of a column. Damian turned his head to me and nodded.

This was definitely one of the batteries. Its toxic signature was unmistakable. The water column above it seemed to shimmer, and trails of mist-like material snaked through the sea as if it were being drawn away.

I shivered. Was this the magic that Matthias was leaching?

Glancing at Damian, I realized that he was still holding his breath. I grabbed his shoulder and reached out with the other arm, creating a bubble of air over his face.

"Thanks." His voice was distorted and muffled in the watery space between us. He smiled at me, and I silently cursed the butterflies that filled my stomach.

Gods, what was becoming of me?

I summoned the jar from the ether and gripped it as tightly as I could. It was supposed to be unbreakable, but I really didn't want to mess this up. Swimming forward, I unscrewed the lid of the jar, but I lifted it only partway. Two inky black worms slithered out, and I rapidly screwed it closed again. We backed up quickly, not wanting to become a target. The worms floated motionless for a few seconds, searching for a magic signature, and then they jetted toward the battery, burrowed into the limestone, and disappeared.

I looked at Damian. "It worked."

"We'll see."

We waited, watching the column base. Chunks of limestone flaked off, and every few seconds, one of the worms' heads broke out of the stone before disappearing again.

Holy crap.

They were literally eating the battery and its magic. Feeling a little guilty, I wondered if there'd be anything left after they depleted the store. The thought of destroying an ancient artifact was disturbing, but considering that it was filled with a shit ton of unstable energy, I decided that it was okay.

A slight movement in my peripheral vision broke me from my hypnotic stare. I glanced behind Damian and noticed a strange eel slither out from two broken stones on the bottom. It looked...odd. Like a second head was growing out of its body, and—

The eel shot forward toward Damian's head, its mouths open. My reflexes surprised me, and I unleashed a jet of air that slammed the eel into a broken lintel.

Damian spun around as the eel slowly sank to the bottom, either dead or knocked unconscious. Now that its entire body was visible, I noticed the strange growths on its sinuous form. It was definitely wrong—mutated, maybe.

He looked at me and shook his head. "The unstable magic has affected the life around here."

Shit. Just what we needed—mutant sea monsters. "Let's hope that Eve's anti-radiation meds will keep us from growing any second limbs," I replied.

A grin pulled at Damian's lips before he looked away. "We can only hope."

I looked around and shivered. What other mutants lurked in the nooks and crannies of these ruins?

After a few minutes, the magic seeping off of the column base visibly lessened. "See that? It's working," Damian said. "The worms are depleting the battery."

Excitement fluttered in my chest, followed by trepidation. This was turning out to be way easier than I'd thought, which, judging by my past record, only meant one thing: the other shoe hadn't yet dropped.

I pushed off the bottom, and my head broke the surface. I just wanted to see what was going on topside. The sun was shining brighter than ever, and I had to squint. Everything seemed normal. No genies. The sky was cloudless. I scanned the shore and—

Ah, shit. There it was. The other shoe.

A strange salamander-like thing was sniffing Damian's backpack. It was the size of a small alligator, and it had a red crest—or a fin?—running along its back. The creature's body suddenly froze, and its head turned toward me, its black eyes locking on to me like a laser.

It tore across the shore in a blur and disappeared into the water, heading right for us.

26

Damian

Neve kicked slowly in the water as I kept my eyes on the battery. The energy was rapidly depleting—I could feel it. The worms weren't simply consuming the magic stored in the battery, but rather devouring the spells that had created the magic in the first place. They were destroying the powerplant, not just the power.

Suddenly, one of Neve's feet kicked me square in the jaw.

Irritation flared, and then my senses pricked. Neve ducked under the water, alarm all over her face. "Incoming!"

I turned just in time to catch the dark shape as it launched out of the shadows. It slammed into my forearm, and I pinned it to the sea floor. Its tail whipped through the water, and one of its razor-sharp barbs sliced my back. I gripped its neck with my free hand and twisted until I felt it snap. The creature's deformed body slackened and went still in the muck.

I looked up at Neve, who was staring at me blankly. "Let's get out of the water. The battery is nearly drained."

She nodded. "What about the other one?"

"We'll get to it. But first, let's make sure there aren't more of those." I gestured to the limp cross between a crocodile and a newt.

Fucking unstable magic.

Our heads broke the surface, and I immediately counted two more of those mutated newts crossing the rocky shoreline.

"Good call," Neve whispered.

I dipped under the water and swam several feet forward into the shallows until I could stand on the bottom. Drawing my bow from the ether, I rose and shot two smoking arrows at the newt closest to us. They hit the target, and the beast hissed...alerting two additional newts, whose heads darted up from a scrubby bush.

As I unleashed another onslaught of arrows, pain ripped through my thigh, and I was pulled under. I dropped my bow, and it disappeared into the ether. Reaching down, I gripped the jaws of the newt who'd sunk its teeth into my flesh. Anger coursed through me, and my dark angel rose. I fought the urge to release it.

The creature's jagged fangs tore through muscle as I pried its mouth open. It released its bite, then twisted furiously under my grip. Flames cascaded from my palms, impervious to the sea, and devoured the mutated creature. In seconds, it was nothing more than a cloud of floating ash.

Clearing the plume with the sweep of my hand, I glanced down at my injured leg. Blood seeped through the water, and my skin slowly knit together.

Too slowly.

Concern tugged at me, but I pushed it aside. Where was Neve?

I stood, my head breaking the surface. Ignoring the throbbing in my shredded muscles, I searched for her.

She was twenty paces away in the shallows, and she had one of the newts levitating six feet in the air. She jerked her arm, and the creature flew into a rock, dying on impact.

Turning her head, she caught sight of me. Fear flashed across her face, then relief. She smiled, and gods be damned, heat rippled through me.

I followed her gaze toward the shore to find three more newts barreling over the bluff toward us. We didn't have time for this. I cut through the water toward them, drawing my blade from the ether.

Suddenly, two flashes crossed the beach, and in their

wake, the newts crumpled to the ground, their heads severed from their bodies.

Every muscle tensed, and I swung around, searching the shore. I sensed them now: Kras and his vampires.

"What the *heck* was that?" Neve's eyes were planted on the dead newts.

"Hello, my darling." Kras appeared on the beach, his trousers and purple dress shirt overly formal for the setting.

My chest rumbled as he grinned at Neve. A newt launched out of the water on my left, and I sliced it in half, all the while watching Kras and his fucking grin.

Kras turned to me and feigned shock. "Oh. You're *still* alive?"

What the hell did he mean by that?

His lascivious gaze returned to Neve. "My, my. You two *are* quite extraordinary."

Two more blurs flashed by, and a pair of mutant newts exploded with a burst of blood, suddenly disemboweled and decapitated.

Valko and Elisa. They were covered head to toe in gore and grinning.

"*Wow*. I haven't had this much fun in over two hundred years." Valko shot Neve and me a deranged smile. "Elisa, can you remember the last time?"

She stooped over a broken column, poking the decapitated body of a newt with a twig, then slowly looked up at Valko and blinked.

"You guys are freaking awesome! Elisa, you were great," Neve said, being far too generous. They were unbelievably fast, yes, but *great* was a stretch.

Kras brushed off his shirt like it had gotten soiled. "Well. After we returned to Sozopol last night, we just *couldn't* sleep. We were so worried."

The way he accentuated certain words sent flames streaking down my palms.

"Very," Elisa said dryly. She dropped the stick she was using to dissect the dead newt, then stood. "We figured you needed some ass-saving."

Neve glanced over at me and grinned. She was clearly growing fond of these vampires.

Just what I needed—spending *more* time with these lunatics.

I sighed and glanced down at my partially healed thigh. Something was wrong with me, and I was certain it had to do with the hydra's poison. I bit back my irritation. "Are you three here to help?"

Kras watched me with hooded eyes, then glanced quickly at Valko and Elisa. A smile broke across his pasty face. "Of course. We are friends now. Plus, we owe you more than you could ever know."

His voice was like nails across a chalkboard, but I glared at him and nodded. I still didn't trust him, and I'd stake him the second he crossed us. But sure, we were friends.

Neve appeared at my side and slid her khanjar into

its sheath. "Let's drain the last battery and get this show on the road."

Her red hair cascaded around her shoulders, and her wet and tattered clothes clung to her soft curves. She was soaked, disheveled, and beaming, and my chest clenched. She was more radiant and confident than ever before.

Somehow, that unleashed a violent surge of emotions and a fierce desire to protect her.

And I would, no matter the cost.

27

Neve

Kras and his vamps patrolled the shore as Damian and I waded into the water, searching for the final battery. This time, we were headed along the other side of the temple, and the water was deeper. It lapped at my chin, and I created another air bubble around my face. Before dipping under, I cast one on Damian, too. He turned back to me, and I caught the flash of flames in his eyes before he sank beneath the waves.

A high-frequency hum filled my ears, and I shivered in the icy water. It was colder here. Was that related to the unstable magic in the batteries?

Damian swam down toward the ruin-filled bottom. Gripping the toppled and broken columns, he pulled himself along, little more than a dark shadow in the murky blue. I followed, trying to ignore the growing pit of unease that had formed in my belly. When he slowed, I peered around his body into the ruins beyond.

Smoky black swirls of energy rose up from the bottom like contrails being pulled out to sea. This was definitely the final battery.

The sea felt greasy and unnatural. This battery's signature was far worse than the other's had been. It tasted like baking soda and sounded like metal brakes grinding. It felt like a fever, too hot and too cold all at once. Nausea overcame me as we swam closer, and it was all I could do not to hurl. It felt like my insides were liquifying...like it was changing me.

We needed to get away from this thing *fast*.

As we drew near, it became clear that the battery was nothing more than a black conical stone, its surface polished like a river rock. It had to have been imported, as I hadn't seen anything like it in the local geology.

I retrieved the jar of magic-eating worms from the ether and swam up beside the stone. The water around the rock distorted my vision. Everything seemed distorted, like when salt and freshwater mix. I gingerly unscrewed the lid and let the remaining two worms slither out. This time, they bolted directly to the stone, imbedded their oily bodies into the black rock, and disappeared. The sight of them made my skin crawl, and I couldn't help but scratch my arm.

This battery was more powerful than the first, and there was no indication that the worms were doing their job.

Damian gripped my shoulder softly, sending heat through me. I suppressed a gasp at the sudden influx of his energy and met his gaze. "Let's return to the surface," he said. "I don't like being so close to this thing. The worms are doing their job, but it will take some time."

Great. He was *definitely* worried about sprouting a third wing, and I didn't blame him. Everything about this magic felt wrong and sickly. I nodded, dismissed the jar, and swam up with him.

When we emerged, Kras was sitting on a rock, while Valko searched the bluff. Elisa had collected the carcasses of the mutated creatures and was setting them on fire. I swam until my feet hit the bottom, then carefully stepped over the jumble of broken architecture.

Kras noticed our return and stood. "That was surprisingly fast work."

"It's not done. We released a spell that's eating away at the magic. It'll be a little while still." I exited the water, extremely disappointed by how horrible my wet clothes and socks felt.

Kras watched me closely with interest, and Damian stepped up beside me, his magic flaring. "We should be ready for Matthias once the power cuts out. Are you prepared to conceal the island once the battery is dead, Krasimir?"

"Absolutely. Dimo is with Luciana as we speak. She is preparing to cast a new spell."

Luciana, I reasoned, must be Kras's sorcerer friend, and Dimo, who knew? Probably another one of Kras's vampires.

"Great." Damian reached into his backpack and pulled out the vial of potion. He took a sip and handed it to me. Though I was feeling better now, I took it anyway.

"Feeling okay?" Kras asked, his eyebrows raised.

"Fine," Damian said coldly.

Was he? He seemed to be acting a little off, but I'd just assumed that was because of what had happened last night. Just the thought of it made warmth pool between my legs and race into my cheeks. I looked up and noticed that Damian was watching me. *Intensely.*

Fates, had Damian noticed that?

Hunger burned in his eyes, and he looked like he wanted to devour me.

Shivers raked my skin, and I looked between Damian and Kras. My life was getting way too weird. I stashed the potion in the bag. There was one dose left, and I hoped we wouldn't need it.

"We should get in position," Damian said.

My stomach dropped. It was time.

The vampires followed us up to the ruins of the colonnaded building, not far from the shore. Damian explained our plan while I selected a spot in the sun not far away. Desperate to get control over my body, I sat on a stone and closed my eyes. The chill of the water was still in my bones, and the sun's rays felt divine. I'd need all the strength I could muster for what was coming.

I summoned the spellbook from the ether, and its powerful magic swirled around me. Working over the spell, I tried to understand its intricate components. While my memory was solid, I still wanted to practice a few more times, just to be ready.

My thoughts drifted to Matthias and his genies. To the djinn. I was drawn to him like a moth to flame. I couldn't describe it. It wasn't sexual attraction, but more like a magnetic force binding us together. Hatred seeped into my veins at the thought of him. He'd caused me so much pain and trouble.

I closed my eyes, imagining my triumph. I would banish him. I would chase him into the Realm of Air and bring his palace crashing down around him. I imagined grinding him down with the stones of his fallen palace and tearing—

Fear prickled my skin.

What the heck was wrong with me?

I wrapped my arms around myself, rubbing my shoulders. My thoughts were deranged. I'd never wanted to kill anybody before, and this sudden desire for violence was frankly terrifying.

Elisabeta appeared beside me and handed me a sucker candy. "I know you'll do it when the time is right."

I craned my neck and looked up at her, confused and surprised. "Do what?"

"Kick some ass." She winked and turned to pick up a mutated flipper lying at the water's edge.

I smiled. Sure, she was a maniac, but I was beginning to like that girl. I stared out at the water, suddenly feeling a boost of confidence. "Yup. I *am* gonna kick some ass."

Damian

I flexed my hand and glanced over at Neve. She was sitting with the spellbook on her lap and watching the water, quiet and pensive. I looked down at my palm. My energy was waning. I'd felt it earlier, but now it was becoming more noticeable. Which meant two things—this was the hydra's poison at work, and it couldn't be cured by a healing potion or my magic. I'd likely need a very specific antidote, and I knew of only one person who might have it: the Apothecary. But there was no time for me to planes-walk back to Magic Side.

"What's that?" Neve's back shot upright, and she jumped to her feet.

I followed her gaze over the water to where the battery was located.

Fuck.

The dark water was churning and bubbling, and streams of magic rose into the air. Something was wrong.

Kras frowned. "Not good, my friends. Not good."

"What does that *mean*, Kras?" Neve said, frustrated.

I watched the water, my concern mounting. "It means the battery is probably weakening. It might explode before the magic is drained."

"Precisely," Kras said. Elisa and Valko moved to his side in a blur. "And that would be extremely bad, my dear. If that battery explodes, we will all be chunks of bone and flesh on this shore. Much like our mutant friends here." Kras glanced at the newt corpses that Elisa had neatly arranged into a pile.

The consequences would be far more dire. An explosion like that would be very difficult to cover up and could risk outing all Magica.

Neve turned to me, a hint of excitement coloring her face. "We could collect the worms from the first battery and put them inside this one. Maybe they can eat the magic before it explodes."

"You have worms? And they eat magic?" Valko knit his brows together and glanced at Kras. "Oh, Kras. We have to hold on to these ones."

I wasn't sure what Valko meant by that, but Neve's idea was good. If my suspicions were correct, though, it was the worms that had weakened the battery. "Too risky. The worms will likely only weaken it further."

"Okay," Neve said, "let's try the opposite approach. Let's use our magic to stabilize the battery."

The vampires looked at Neve, then at me. "That *could* work. But if it doesn't, you'll be fish food," Kras said.

Directing magic into the battery might stabilize it. It was insanely dangerous, but it was the only option we had right now. "I'll do it. Neve, if this goes wrong, you'll need to planes-walk everyone out instantly. Take cover and go at the first sign that it's not working."

Neve shot me a deadly glare. "Not a chance. I'm coming with you."

Frustration blazed through me. She was one of the few who openly defied me, time and time again. I didn't want to put her at risk, but there would be no changing her mind once she'd set its course.

"Fine," I grumbled.

"Well, it was great catching up. Glad we could help. But I think we'll be leaving now," Kras said cheerfully.

I felt the flames burn inside me. "Thanks for your help."

"We'll see you soon." Valko waved. "Hopefully."

Then the three of them disappeared like the wind. Fucking vampires.

The sky above us had become stormy. Dark clouds

circled overhead, as if drawn to the magic of the unstable battery.

I glared at Neve. "I don't like any of this."

"I know. Too bad. I'm coming."

"Planes-walk at the first sign of trouble."

She just gave me an icy stare and crafted masks of air over our mouths.

I cut through the water and dove under. Neve was close behind—I felt her signature even with the battery's overwhelming magic. Her presence helped focus my mind. The battery's magic was unstable and sickly, but it still called to me.

My FireSoul curse.

It was hard enough having to fight the dark angel. Doing it while taming the dragon was becoming nearly impossible. Not to mention, I was growing weaker by the minute.

I pushed aside the sickly worry. Worry was weakness.

Up ahead, the water glowed a blinding blue. It burned my eyes just looking at it.

The signature of its magic had changed to a maddening cacophony of scents and sensations. I could feel it poisoning my blood, and my throat started to swell.

I swung around to face Neve. The water around us was pulsing with the eerie light, greasy and foul, making it difficult to see even a few feet away. Her eyes were bloodshot and releasing red tears, and she was struggling to swim forward.

I had healing magic, however compromised. She did not.

This wasn't worth it.

Fuck the battery. Fuck the Order. Fuck Matthias and his genies.

It was time to get out.

Neve

Damian pulled on my arm and pointed toward the shore. "Go."

Frustration mixed with nausea, and I shook my head. I was going to fix this damn thing.

I released a thin stream of magic toward the battery, testing. I couldn't see the battery itself, just the strange, pulsing glow. We were too far away, but I knew in the pit of my stomach that getting any closer would mean certain death.

The sea rumbled, and the light intensified as a fresh wave of nauseating power washed over us. My body shook with sickness.

Damian firmly gripped my arm. "We'll find another way."

Frustration welled up in my throat. This was all going to shit, and this magic was killing us.

Damian looked pale and sickly in a way I had never seen. There were open wounds on his leg and back that should have closed. Was this corruption affecting his ability to heal?

Okay. That was it. We'd find another way.

I kicked hard toward the shore. My limbs were heavy, but with every stroke forward, a little of the nausea left.

By the time we reached the shallows, the unnaturally icy water felt practically rejuvenating, though it was probably still toxic as heck. Thank fates we had some potion left.

I stood and staggered forward, breathing hard.

Damian craned his head skyward. "Fuck."

I followed his gaze. The whole sky had turned into a spinning storm of dark clouds. I looked back. The water over the battery boiled violently, and luminescent plumes of magic spiraled upward.

What had we done?

I opened my mouth to speak, and then the world turned upside down.

28

Neve

The sea around us rushed out in a violent torrent. My body crashed against the rocks, and pain flared from a thousand cuts.

Damian tumbled through the water beside me. I tried to catch his hand, but we were yanked apart by the current.

With a deafening roar, the water vanished, dropping us onto the slime-covered stones of the seabed. I braced for another impact, but nothing came. The waves hung suspended in air, as if time had stopped.

Pain throbbed in my side—a bruised rib, probably.

I dismissed the bubble of air around my face and looked up, immediately swaying with vertigo as I took in the sight. Waves rose around us on three sides, creating a watery prison.

"You idiots."

My heart skipped a beat at the sound of Matthias's voice behind us. I scrambled to my feet and turned, barely able to keep my balance in the slime and rubble. It didn't help that I was still queasy from our proximity to the battery.

Matthias stood on the rocky shore. The marid loomed above him, riding the back of a serpent formed from the sea itself.

The air left my lungs as I gazed into the marid's infinitely blue eyes. His signature roared over me like thunder, overwhelming my senses. Amid the stench of marine growth, I caught an earthy scent of old wood and tobacco and the taste of salt and sweet herbs. With his outstretched hands, he appeared to be controlling the looming waves, wielding the walls of water like an executioner wields an axe.

"What in fates have you done?" Matthias screamed.

I shot him the finger. "We just shoved a stick in your bicycle spokes! Your magic batteries are history, so you can kiss your little demi-plane goodbye."

"My gods." His eyes widened, and he staggered back. "You fools don't know what you're dealing with! Do you have any idea how much danger we're all in?"

"Well, I assume a lot less danger than your demon army would be," Damian said, his voice like thunder.

Matthias flicked his hand, and the marid released the sea.

Watching the water around us drop, I froze for half a second before instinct kicked in and my wits returned. I summoned a wall of wind, deadening the impact of the waves and buying us just enough time to take flight before they crashed together.

Matthias screamed in rage and rose on demon wings.

The marid surged upward on his water serpent, but he couldn't fly like we could. He was chained to the sea.

That was something, at least.

Scanning the sky, I found no sign of the djinn. Anger swelled in my chest. I'd hoped to get them both, but the marid was the crucial one. If I could banish him, the curse would be lifted from Bentham.

I circled back to Damian's side. "So much for surprise. Keep your creepy friend off me while I blast Fish Face out of here."

Damian summoned his spear in one hand. "Gladly."

I pulled the spellbook from the ether and began reciting the banishment spell. The magic from the book poured through me, demanding to be released. Unfortunately, the spell was long and tortuous, as powerful spells often were.

Damian soared through the air, heading straight for Matthias. He dismissed his spear and unleashed a torrent of fire.

Matthias burst up out of the explosion, cursing and quickly flapping his wings to extinguish the flame. Damian tucked his wings and spun, narrowly avoiding the pillar of water that the marid launched skyward.

"Bastard!" I swore and dashed through the air behind the marid. I just needed him distracted for a few more seconds.

Agony suddenly quaked through my body as something slammed into me, driving the wind from my lungs. I spiraled downward, head over heels, and the book tumbled out of my hands. Cursing, I dismissed it only feet before it could plunge into the water.

Then I felt him. The vile taste of his magic seeping into my skin like a poison.

The *fucking* djinn.

His laughter shook the air around me, and I twisted, searching the empty sky.

Then the sea exploded upward, forming into watery fingers that plucked Damian from the air and pulled him beneath the waves.

"No!" Terror clenched my heart, and I soared across the water, searching for Damian. A tornado slammed into me, but I countered the force with a burst of wind that stopped me from crashing into the churning ocean.

The djinn was on me in seconds.

I dodged his grasp just as Damian's hand broke the surface of the water. Grabbing his wrist with both hands, I shot skyward as fast as I could, towing him along. His shoulder popped, and he growled with rage. Somehow, he managed to reach up and grip my arm with his free hand, releasing some of the weight on his dislocated shoulder.

Gods, that must be painful.

I silently cringed as I shot a quick glance over my shoulder.

Fuck!

The djinn soared behind us on a billowing cloud of smoke. But worse, dark clouds filled the sky, swirling around us. I could sense they weren't the djinn's doing, but rather the corrupted magic of the unstable battery building into a storm. Judging by the rapidly increasing wind currents that jarred me, we didn't have much time.

Damian squeezed my arm. "It's time to get rid of these assholes. Banish the marid. I'll handle the djinn."

Before I could respond, he flipped backward and dove, spear in hand. At point-blank range, he hurled the weapon into the djinn's chest. The spear exploded in a ball of fire, like a lightning bolt hitting the earth.

My nemesis screamed, and joy flooded my heart. I wanted to finish him, to unleash my magic, but my better sense prevailed.

First, the marid. He controlled the curse.

With a burst of speed, I darted toward the sea, summoning the spellbook from the ether. Its magic flowed into me again, and I started reciting the spell as soon as the marid was in range.

He turned his blue eyes on me and roared in fury, clearly sensing my intention. A geyser of water erupted in my direction, but I twisted out of the way, never stopping my words.

The marid cursed and threw himself into the sea, and the churning waters stilled.

He was gone. I no longer felt the tug of his magic entwined with the spell. Had he planes-walked, or was he lurking beneath the waves?

Well, shit.

I coasted close to the water, trying to lure the marid to strike, but the sea remained calm.

Suddenly, explosions drew my attention above. The djinn was still here, and Damian...was in trouble.

Lightning bolts cracked through the air around Damian, making the situation crystal clear. We had to take out one of these bastards, or everything would be for naught. I left the sea behind and soared toward the battle in the sky.

Book in hand, I recited the spell again as Damian strafed the djinn with bolts of fire. Consumed in battle, Damian spiraled dangerously close to the island in a dance of fire and wind.

My spell started to take hold, and I chanted faster...

A sonic boom slammed into my body and deafened me. Damian's body convulsed, and he rocketed out of control. My heart leapt to my throat, and every part of my soul cried out, as I chased the djinn downward.

Damian righted himself just above the ground, but the djinn was on him in a second. A blast of wind drove Damian into the dirt.

Rage consumed me, and I screamed the final words of the spell. My words sliced through the air like lightning, and the magic leapt from my body into a whirling vortex.

The djinn looked back.

Bye-bye, asshole.

The banishment spell consumed him in a crackling whirlwind. His screams of rage echoed in my ears as he vanished in a thunderous boom, permanently exiled from our world.

Waves of exhaustion flowed over me, followed by relief. The djinn was gone. *Banished.* He would no longer be able to come for me or my friends. But I was too tired to feel true elation. My muscles screamed, and I had to find Damian.

My chest tight with worry, I soared along the coastline, searching for signs of life. Where was he? And where the *heck* was Matthias?

Suddenly, a blinding light flashed offshore, and a wave of corrupted magic washed over me, knocking me off balance. I had to choke back the nausea to keep from retching.

Shit.

The final battery had just gone Chernobyl.

Damian

My body slammed into the ground, and my ribs shattered. I rolled left, gasping. It would have been worse if I hadn't stopped my fall before that last blast.

I steadied myself with my hands on the shards of marble as the earth spun around me and the ringing in my ears abated. I tried to get my bearings, but the impact left me disoriented and dizzy. Ruined columns lay around me. A deafening burst of thunder exploded.

Ears ringing again, I scanned the sky overhead, but there was no sign of Neve or the djinn.

Matthias appeared on my left, dropping to the earth on dark, leathery wings.

I staggered to my feet and wiped the blood from my eyes, my rage drowning out the pain. I growled and charged forward, unleashing a rain of fire and ice.

Matthias leapt to the side, drew an iron spear, and hurled it at me. Using his mastery over iron, he guided it like a missile.

I summoned my blade and deflected the spear with ease before dismissing it into the ether. He could control my weapons just as well as I could control his.

Matthias laughed and threw a handful of nails into the air. They exploded outward like a hail of bullets, and

I dove for cover behind a marble column as they rico-cheted off the stones around me.

Then a mind-wrenching clanging reverberated from the shore. I lifted my head just as a horde of barnacle-encrusted chains slithered out of the water, animated like snakes. Their heads were comprised of forked anchors, abandoned by passing ships. The bastard must have summoned them from their watery slumber with his iron magic.

The chains rattled across the broken ground with blinding speed.

Fuck.

Releasing my wings, I leapt into the air and fired a blast of hail at Matthias. A wall of water shot between us, blocking the ice.

The marid.

Matthias threw his hands up, and the anchor chains shot skyward like grapnels. I tucked my wings and spun out of the way, but my body lurched as a crusty chain wrapped around my ankle. A second wrapped around my wing.

I will not be chained again.

I unleashed a torrent of fire at the chain around my ankle, and it released its hold. But I struggled to gain altitude as more chains shot after me, wrapping around my legs and towing me to the ground.

I could planes-walk, but as soon I left, Matthias and his genies would almost certainly turn their focus on

Neve. I scanned the sky for her as I struggled against the chains, falling several feet. Where *was* she?

"Neve!" I shouted. "Go now!"

I prayed to the cursed fates that she could hear me. I didn't have much time.

The wind exploded from my lungs, and agony lanced through my chest as a sharp anchor barb lodged itself in my ribcage. I sucked in a breath, producing the horrific sound of gurgling blood.

Bolts of pain cut through my thigh, my stomach, and my chest as more grapnels hauled me to the earth. My body, wrapped in iron, slammed onto the broken marble pavement of the temple. My vision went red as agony rocked me, and blood poured from my mouth as I gasped for air.

I couldn't heal with the hydra's poison in my veins, and with these wounds, I wouldn't survive the rigors of planes-walking. Even if I did live through the trip, I was too much of a pincushion to do anything but instantly bleed out on arrival.

Fuck. I'd missed my shot.

Matthias appeared in my blurry vision, and rage coursed through my veins. I unleashed a wall of fire, but it dissipated in an explosion of steam as the marid countered it with a thin sheet of water. The chains constricted, and more blood welled up.

I was growing weak.

"Well, well, what do we have here?" Matthias said,

kneeling beside me. His eyes betrayed no fear, only deep weariness and ruthless calculation. He tugged on one of the chains. "An ancient smith and master of fire chained to the ground. Do you fancy yourself a modern-day Prometheus, Damian? I guess that makes me Zeus."

"That makes you a—"

The chains tightened, crushing my ribs, and I choked on the rising blood.

"I am sorry, old friend," Matthias said, resentment infecting his words. "But you have done more damage to the world than you could ever know. And this is your punishment."

"I'll see you in hell."

"Very probably. I go there frequently these days. They're very open to new ideas. I was going to tell you about it, even bring you on board. But somehow, you decided to defect to the other side at the worst time possible."

"When did you go mad? Helping devils and demons?"

The anchors dug in further as Matthias's eyes filled with anger. "How *dare* you help the Order after everything we went through together!"

"They're not the Watchers, Matthias."

"They're just as bad, just weaker and short-sighted. Their vision is no different—a world where Magica live in chains. Bright flowers, doomed to die without sunlight."

"I thought you gave up your delusions years ago."

"Not all of us are as adept at self-deception or at giving up on things as you are. The question now is, do you have what it takes to save yourself?"

"I'll kill you with my dying breath." I struggled against the chains as the world grew soft around the edges. Though I summoned my magic, it was no use.

Matthias leaned in close and whispered, "You can save yourself, you know. Your genie will be here in seconds. She will find you at death's door. All you have to do *is wish*. I think she'd go for that one."

"Never."

"We'll see. Either way, I win."

Then he was gone.

29

Neve

Lightning bolts of wild magic danced over the boiling water, and the maelstrom around us took on an evil green light.

Holy smokes, this was bad. The battery had just gone nuclear, and if I didn't want to grow fifty tentacles, we had to get out.

How much time did we even have?

Matthias flew from the ruins of the temple, the marid at his side.

Not much, guessing by the speed at which *they* were moving.

They didn't see me, thank fates.

I cursed. This could have been my chance. But I was

far too exhausted, the spellbook was drained, the last magic battery just detonated, and we were all going to be irradiated shortly. Time was up.

I scanned the wreckage below, searching for Damian, but there was nothing but blood and iron chains.

My heart clenched. That was a bad sign.

Matthias looked up and spotted me. Rising on dark wings, he screamed, "You! You've no idea what work you have undone! I will make you pay dearly for this!"

I rocketed down from the sky, a cyclone of wind spinning around me, ready to destroy.

With a flick of his wrist, Matthias disappeared, along with the marid.

And shock slammed into my chest. They were gone, and the island was about to turn into Atlantis. I needed to find Damian.

Releasing the winds around me, I slowed my descent. A slight movement caught my eye.

"Damian!"

No answer.

Panic raked my skin as I landed hard and raced to his crumpled body, nearly twisting my ankle on the rubble. *Fates, please.*

Slime-coated chains snaked around his body, and blood was seeping from where the hooks of anchors had dug into his chest and legs.

My heart split, and a cry escaped my mouth.

No. No. No.

The world spun, but I fought the vertigo and knelt at his side. "Damian?"

His head rolled toward me, eyes unfocused. "Did you get the djinn?"

"Yes. Now, be quiet while I pull these out."

"No. It's too much." He reached up and gripped my wrist, his words whispers.

"You'll heal."

"Not this time. The hydra's poison. Get to safety. Get to the Order. They will protect you. There's no time. Go. Now."

I grabbed his cold hand. "The battery just blew. I'll planes-walk us out of here. Ethan can heal you."

He slowly rolled his head back and forth. "I won't make it. You have to go without me. Save yourself."

The truth of his words hit me like a semi, and I choked back tears. His hands were ice, his skin pale. He'd lost too much blood and was probably septic from the marine filth. Death had sunk her claws into him and wasn't letting go.

"No." My heart raged against my chest. I might not love him, but *fates be damned*, I couldn't live without him.

A spark of hope flickered in my mind. Maybe there was a way I could undo this.

I grabbed his jaw and turned his face to meet my eyes. "You have to make a wish. I can save you, Damian. *Make a wish.*"

"No."

"Damian, are you insane? Wish it now!"

"No. It's what Matthias wants. What he planned. He left me as bait. If I make a wish, you become a djinn, and he binds you. It's a trap."

I cursed as tears finally broke free.

"I don't care. I'll be powerful enough to protect myself from him. And I'll have you there at my side to protect me. You could even make another wish, wish him away."

"He's waiting for it. I will not make you his slave," he said, his eyes growing milky.

"You bastard! Make the fates-damned wish!"

"It's time for you to go, Neve. You'll die if you don't get out of this corrupted magic."

Anger surged through me, and I dug my fingers into his jaw.

"Screw you, Damian Malek. I wish to heal you! I *wish* to heal you!"

He smiled. "I don't think it works that way. Let me go, Neve."

Frustration and despair shook my body. I knew that djinn couldn't grant their own wishes, but I couldn't accept that. I was *not* letting go of him.

I slid my hands through the chains and rested them his chest, trying to pour my magic into him. "I wish to heal you!"

Damian's lips pulled up again into a heart-wrenching smile, and his head slumped back, the last flickering light draining from his eyes.

Fear, sorrow, and primal rage tore through me, and I screamed, "I WISH TO HEAL YOU!"

My words sounded strange in my ears, like echoes disappearing in a canyon. They hadn't even been words, but the song of creation itself. The unwritten language that had once divided day from night, that had divided the sky and the land and the sea.

And in that moment, I saw all of reality as it had ever been. As it ever *could* be.

I saw Damian alive, whole again, smiling back at me.

I reached for that vision, and power surged through my body. My tattoo erupted in white flames as magic flowed across my skin, and I pushed my magic down into Damian's chest.

With a crack, his ribs knit beneath my hands. The chain and anchors around him dissolved into rust. His eyes snapped open, and he gasped in shock and pain.

My body shook as the swell of power flowed through me. I was alive, *truly* alive for the first time in my life.

I was me.

Damian reached out a hand, but I wasn't done. I had seen what could be—what *I* could be.

I would heal it all.

I poured my magic into the world as if I were an endless decanter of power, limitless and radiant like the sun.

In my vision, I had seen the temple as it once had been. I took that fragment of reality, and I healed the temple, too. Suddenly, the columns and rubble and dust around us rose into the air. The dust swirled on the wind, making the stones whole. They reassembled, and the temple rose on all sides of us like it once had been centuries ago.

But I wasn't done. I pushed life back into the withered plants around us, and the island turned green. I pulled the corrupted magic from the air, then dove beneath the waves, healing the shattered statues, the ruptured battery.

Above the waves, the maelstrom still raged, and lightning cracked around the temple...so I would heal the sky, too. I exploded upward from the waters and transformed in a whirling cyclone. I breathed in lightning, feeling its power crackle within me. A raging torrent of wind, I turned clockwise against the hurricane, grinding against it, slowing it moment by moment.

Then the storm collapsed, drained of its power. The clouds dissipated, and blue sky emerged.

Only Damian and I remained.

All this I did in one second. In a single breath.

I surveyed the world I had restored—a green island, resting in the glistening sea. The roofs of ancient buildings dotted the hillside. I hadn't just healed the temple, but the entire city.

And Damian.

Damian

Rage tore through my chest.

What had she done?

I prayed to the heavens, the fates, the gods, that she hadn't made a wish. My life wasn't worth the cost, and that cost would be dear.

I cursed and rolled to my side, finally free of the crushing weight of the chains.

If only that friend of hers was here. If only I could reverse time.

Desperation pulled me to my feet, and I gasped, bracing myself against a newly standing column. Neve had healed me completely, but my body still remembered the wounds: shattered ribs, impaled by rusted iron, betrayed more deeply than ever before.

I could barely see through my anger and pain. I growled, shook it off, and strode out through the columned temple and down the marble stairs.

An ancient city stood around me, empty of inhabitants but perfectly preserved. Wonder flowed through me. What *had* she done? The landscape around us was green, no longer the drab gray and brown of withered plants, and the sky was clear.

Had we traveled through time?

Neve floated down out of the sky, white light curling up from her eyes like spirals of smoke. Her tattoo blazed across her body, her clothes no longer able to mask it. Her signature thundered around me, threatening to crush me like the pressure of the deep. Never had it been so strong. It no longer just smelled like hints of citrus and jasmine, but now was like waking from sleep in a flower-lined orchard, so soft and aromatic it made my head spin. It sounded like the soft cry of distant birds and tasted pure and fresh like the wind before a rainstorm. Her magic felt like standing at the edge of a precipice. Not vertigo, but that irresistible urge to step into the sky and fall forever.

Never had I craved anything so much.

"You're alive!" She wrapped her arms around me.

Her magic was so strong, it nearly choked me. I wanted to scream and shove her from me in fury at what she had done, but I couldn't resist her power. I buried my face in her flowing red hair, breathing in the scents of her body.

She was a drug I could no longer resist. I was out of my mind, consumed with desire. I grasped her back with my hands and pulled her tightly against me.

Neve inhaled sharply at my touch. She yanked my head from her neck and kissed me, biting at my lips as she entwined her arms around me. Her kiss was soft and warm and passionate...but also different. She had been reborn—still the same person, but also someone new, something more.

I fought for clarity as we kissed. At last, when I had seized control of my body, I pushed her away. "Neve," I gasped, "what have you done?"

She winked. "I made a wish. I'm a genie, you know."

"No! How is that even possible?" Fear coursed through me, and the world spun. I braced myself and looked up at her.

Worry tugged at the corners of her eyes. "I don't know. It's not supposed to be possible. I don't really understand anything about my powers. Maybe it worked because I made the wish to save you, and not for myself?"

"Shit!" I grabbed her by the shoulders. "You played right into Matthias's hand. You should have let me die. That's what I *wanted*. That was my wish. Now that you're a genie, he can trap you, *bind* you. This is exactly what he planned!"

Rage consumed Neve's face. "How dare you yell at me for saving your life!" She shoved my hands away from her shoulders and burst into a brightly glowing light, then gestured to her glowing form. "This? This is what *I* wanted. My inheritance. My power. My right. My wish."

I staggered back as her signature exploded around her, overwhelming my senses. But it didn't calm my fear.

Summoning my blade, I scanned the sky and hills around us. Where was he?

I grabbed for her hand, but she pulled it away. "Matthias can bind you now," I said. "Like we bound the djinn."

"Let him try." A malicious smile crossed her face, and her voice took on a strange echo. "I will dissolve every bone in his body. I will grind him to dust."

My heart clenched. I knew that emotion well. The rage, the hatred—they echoed the voice of the djinn and the voice of my soul. My dark angel rose in response to her siren call, ready to follow Neve down a path of fury and destruction.

Ready to destroy the world for vengeance.

But where had that gotten me in the past?

I fought against the darkness, blow by blow, like a boxer frantically punching above his weight, driven by the desperation of the moment. One of us had to remain in control. And Neve was drunk with new magic. I knew that feeling, too, and it wasn't easy to shake.

My breathing steadied, and I reached out to touch her, but she recoiled, still raging. I had to make peace. "I'm sorry that I put you at risk. But thank you. Thank you for saving my life."

She glared.

"I will earn your gift. I will protect you."

Her eyes narrowed in on mine. "I don't need your

protection. I can protect myself, thank you very much. I am as a goddess now."

"Yes. A goddess that might end up captured and bound to the service of an evil man. We were able to capture the djinn. Who knows what demonic tricks Matthias is capable of?"

Her muscles tensed, betraying her deep-seated fear —one that had made her hide her identity for a decade.

I scanned the sky again. "What happened to Matthias and his genies? If they're not here hunting you, then where are they?"

She shook her head as if dispelling a lingering dream. When she looked up, the fire in her eyes had died down, and lucidity had returned. "I'm not sure. I chased him away. He said he was going to make us pay."

I nodded. "Then probably Magic Side. We need to stop him before he unleashes hell on the city."

30

Neve

Emotion tore at me like a whirlwind: rage, frustration, fear, elation.

Relief.

Damian was okay. I was a genie. Matthias was on the loose.

It was all too much to process, so I focused on one thought: vengeance.

Anger burned in my heart like an unstable sun. I'd never had power like this before. Not a fraction. I drank it in like flowing wine. It coursed through my veins and burned my skin, and I loved every agony of it.

I would destroy Matthias. I would take my magic

and rip apart the atoms of his body. Euphoria overwhelmed me.

I snatched the exhausted spellbook from the ground and grabbed Damian by the shoulder. "Let's go."

Before he could respond, the cosmos exploded around us. It was no longer the strange and alien expanse I had once fought so hard to navigate. It was mine to traverse, for I knew the song of creation.

Something flickered at the edge of my perception. As my being expanded outward, I sensed that dark place to which I couldn't travel. Claustrophobia overwhelmed me as I grazed it with my mind. I could taste the choking dust and suffocating air.

The poisoned Realm of Earth, *my contrary plane.*

Screw it. The rest of the universe was mine.

I focused on Magic Side, and we were there. No whirling, no vertigo, just instantaneous travel.

We snapped into reality outside of Bentham Prison.

Water flowed into my mouth as a wave rolled over us, knocking me off balance into a chunk of crumbled masonry.

Damian grabbed my arm, and our heads surged up out of the churning water that had washed over the shore.

The marid is here.

After a few blinks, my vision cleared, and I saw him.

He rose on a massive tendril of water, slamming wave after wave into the walls of the prison.

The curse had done its damage. The entire dome flickered. Only the ruins that were still under the protection spell remained, but they, too, were completely infected with black lines. The panopticon was laced with dark magic as well.

Screaming bluecoats struggled in the waves as they surged through the prison grounds. Some brave souls were flying, casting spells, trying to repel the marid's attack. Were my friends among them?

The marid unleashed torrential rain and streams of water at the defenders while the raging sea did its work.

"Time to take the bastard out of the game." I turned to Damian, who was watching me closely, concern etched across his features.

He nodded. "Lead the charge."

I soared across the water, feeling my magic surge. The marid spotted me and wheeled, fury burning in his infinitely blue eyes.

"You." His voice echoed across the water, grinding the hulls of boats against the rocks.

I could feel his power, but it was nothing compared to mine. Magic swirled within me, desperately trying to tear its way out.

I wouldn't need the spellbook this time. *I* was the reservoir of power.

I spoke the incantation, but once again, I didn't recognize my own voice. Instead of laboring through the long and complex language of the spell, my tongue unconsciously wove all the intricacies of the spell into a single word.

"BEGONE."

Power erupted out of me, and the marid screamed in defiance. A churning vortex of water rose in the sky behind him, a portal to the Realm of Water. He fought against it, clawing toward me, but the portal collapsed around him, devouring him whole.

Then the waves stilled, and the sky cleared.

I wheeled around. Water poured out of the ruined prison grounds, but the inky tendrils of the devouring curse faded into mist and drifted away.

A heavy sigh escaped my lungs as exhaustion overtook me. Never had I felt so depleted, as if all of my magic had gone with the spell.

But we'd won.

I started to drift back across the water, heading for the prison and my friends.

"Well done."

The voice itched my skin, and I whirled, coming face to face with Matthias.

And his host of demons.

He grinned. "You must be utterly exhausted from that spell."

Fear tore through me, a rampant beast. I was weak, exposed, and alone.

Triple shit.

Damian streaked across the water, burning blade in

hand. Matthias flicked his wrist, and the cloud of demons descended on him, whirling savage chains above their heads.

"I have something of yours, Neve." My head snapped back at the sound of Matthias's voice. He raised my old khanjar.

Confusion froze me, and then my blood iced.

An object precious to me. To use in a binding spell. The bastard had been planning this moment for a long time, just as Damian had warned.

Matthias began the familiar incantation, the one I had used to bind the djinn in the Realm of Air. The spell pulled at me, digging away at my magic with foul claws.

"Get out of here, Neve!" Damian swooped in and grabbed a demon by the neck, severing its wing with a savage hack of his black blade. It screeched, and Damian spun away, narrowly missing the barbed chains thrown by the demon's allies.

Rage tore through me, and I unleashed a blast of wind at Matthias. But it was little more than a breeze, and he barely bothered to dodge it.

I was tired. Slow. Completely exhausted.

Fear welled up in my throat as Matthias's incantation wound around me like a net, draining my strength. I now understood the djinn's horrid screams when I'd bound him. To be robbed of power in this way was to be defiled. Guilt and fear twined in my chest, strangling me.

"Neve, go!"

But my rage returned, refusing to relinquish control. I charged, releasing bolt after bolt of wind, but Matthias deftly spun away, barely disturbed by the passing gusts.

I couldn't hear Matthias's voice over the rush of wind, but I felt the spell tightening around my throat. Soon, I wouldn't even be able to breathe. I grasped at my neck, and my fingers brushed the cold metal that was forming there—a magical collar.

Chained.

Panic overcame me, and I couldn't think.

I had to run.

I tried to planes-walk, but Matthias's words were like anchors, pulling me down.

Trapped and chained. A servant to him.

Damian conjured a wall of flame to shield me from the demons. He rammed a smoking spear through one demon's chest, trying desperately to fight his way to Matthias.

Panic drove me onward. I shot across the water, trying to make it to Bentham, to the Order. Surely they could protect me...

Despair and pain churned in my blood. The further I flew, the stronger the bonds tightened, closing my throat.

I choked out a scream for help.

And then the sky turned orange as a flaming meteor

ripped out of the clouds. It slammed into Matthias, driving his body into the water.

The shackles of the spell around me shattered, and I relished the air that filled my lungs.

Holy shit. Had I called down a meteor?

I spun around to see the meteor still floating above the water. My heart leapt as it uncoiled into a shimmering red dragon. Flames erupted from its mouth as it sprayed the surface of the lake where Matthias had fallen, and then it turned on the demons. They scattered into the air and vanished in puffs of dark smoke, dragon fire licking at their heels. The dragon then flew back and forth, skimming the water, searching. But Matthias and his demons were gone.

"Spark?" I whispered.

The dragon turned to me with blazing eyes.

I am almost big enough to eat him now, but I don't think he would taste good.

"Spark!" Elation filled my chest.

Spark swept the waves with another shower of flame. *I think he has gone away. I do not sense his essence.*

I soared through the air and instinctively wrapped my arms around Spark's neck. Surprise raced across my skin. I could touch him now, though he was still semi-translucent. "Spark, you're like... a somewhat larger dragon?"

I am a large dragon. It's our bond. You have become very powerful, so I have grown.

He drew in a breath and puffed his chest out, and though I was rapidly losing altitude due to exhaustion, I couldn't help but smile. "I need a rest, Spark. I've never been so tired."

Climb on. You need to eat something with good essence. Like Chicago Dogs.

My stomach growled, and I felt a jolt of energy.

"That sounds wonderful. But first, we need to get Damian."

Damian

I shoved my spear deeper into the demon, just to watch the light in its eyes go out.

It gurgled and gasped and tumbled into the waves. But there was no satisfaction in the kill. Soon, it would dissolve into smoke and rejoin Matthias in hell. Or wherever he was. There was no victory in killing demons, just endless toil.

Would that it had been Matthias sliding off my spear. As a half-demon, he would also be reborn—though perhaps differently, more demonically. Perhaps it had already happened. Perhaps that explained his change.

Spark—the dragon who was not a dragon—wheeled

over the water to Neve's side. He was far larger now, maybe fifteen feet long, though still a wyrmling by some standards.

Jealousy rippled through me as Neve put her arms around him. Jealousy and a haunting sense of failure. Clearly, I couldn't protect her, but he could.

"We did it, Damian." Neve smiled at me, and my heart broke.

Exhausted, she collapsed onto Spark's back. They wheeled into the air and started across the glistening water toward Bentham Island, and I followed beside them.

They shared a bond. Knew each other's thoughts.

Of course, I shared a bond with Neve, too. One driven by craving. There was no question now. Even exhausted, her signature drove me mad with desire. Her power was a sweet nectar, and I wanted nothing more than to consume it with all my being. She was so strong now. The vibrations of her power were like a thundering storm, drowning out my thoughts.

I drew near, and she turned and spoke to me. But I couldn't make out her words over the maelstrom in my mind, so I flew on in silence beneath the shroud of my failure.

It wasn't just her power that drew me. I desired *her* as well. It raged in my heart against the craving in my soul. I wanted to lift Neve into the air and kiss her deeply. I wanted to take her away and lay her down in soft sheets and fall into her embrace.

But I knew I couldn't trust myself. My blackened soul craved more than she could give. I could fight against it, but it would constantly be whispering in my ear, *take it all.*

Eventually, I was bound to slip. She'd risked everything to bring me back from the brink of death, and now I was as deadly a threat to her as Matthias was.

Where there should have been rage, there was only despair.

We alighted on the ruins of the prison. The chaos barely registered. I only had eyes for Neve, like a leopard watching its prey, like a vampire mesmerized by an accidental drop of blood.

Neve's boss nodded in my direction and said something. Rhiannon said something as well. Cops were shouting back and forth around us, all meaningless, unintelligible murmuring. I only heard the crying of birds on the wind. There was only citrus and rain and jasmine. And I wanted it all.

Anger tore at me. Why was I cursed this way? Born as a FireSoul and driven to kill and steal magic. Reborn as a fallen angel and tortured by rage.

It was too much. Even though I had learned to handle the rage, my FireSoul magic was like the marid's devouring curse, eating me from the inside out. Soon, it would consume me and everything I loved and touched.

I stepped back as Neve hugged her friends. She didn't hide her signature now. The thing she feared most had come to pass.

And it was my fault. My weakness. Matthias had used me as a snare, and now she was more vulnerable than ever before.

Spark swung his head back and forth, vigilantly scanning the prison.

Resentment crawled along my skin. I couldn't even protect Neve from myself.

A throbbing ache grew in my chest as I realized what had to be done.

Get away from her. Forever. That was the only solution.

Find Matthias. Find a way to destroy him.

And take the power to do it.

31

Neve

Rhiannon squeezed her arms around me. Her familiar honeysuckle signature cut through everything else, all my worries and fears.

Except the damp. *That* persisted. We were both soaked head to toe, and Rhiannon was shivering in my arms. I drew on my weakened magic and my bond with Spark to make a warm breeze around us.

Rhiannon breathed a sigh of relief. "Gods, that feels nice."

I squeezed her harder, and stepped back, letting the air dryer do its work. "I'm so glad you're safe," I said. "You look like you lost an argument with a washing machine."

"I'm lucky I didn't split my skull open. But you...you did it, you banished the freaking marid!"

Gretchen crossed her arms. "And just in the nick of time, too. You saved our asses. Thank you."

Water dripped from Gretchen's tattered clothes, and her bedraggled hair lay tangled around her shoulders. There were bits of turf in it, and she bore a ton of scratches. Lily and Ethan had fared no better.

I expanded the warm air around us all, but some of my joy left me. "We didn't get Matthias."

"You crippled him by banishing the marid, and you broke the curse. That was the job. Taking him down is the next step, which we'll do *together*." Rhiannon stepped back to study me. "You've changed."

I glanced nervously at the gathered faces. For the most part, it was just my friends—Gretchen, Rhiannon, Lily, and Ethan. And Damian, standing far back.

A trickle of panic raced over my skin, but I forced it down. I was done hiding, at least from my friends.

"I think I may have granted a teensy, tiny, little wish, and now, apparently, I'm a full djinn."

Gretchen raised her eyebrows. "I'll be damned."

"Holy shit, Neve! That's amazing. And boy, do I have a laundry list of wishes for you"—Rhiannon looked down at her backside—"starting with these."

I shoved her hard with a grin. "I wouldn't change a freckle on your face!"

"Can you really grant wishes?" Ethan asked.

Fear iced my skin. I barely knew him, and now he —*they*—knew my deepest secret. In the moment, they had been part of my team, but really, Rhiannon was the only one I trusted with my life. And Damian.

"I...I don't know. I need to work that out. But I'm serious, you can tell no one." I looked at Gretchen, narrowing my eyes. "Not even the Order. I'm in enough danger from Matthias as it is."

My heart raced, and I touched my neck where the bonds of his spell had choked me. My worst nightmare coming true, moment by moment. I fought back the urge to flee.

"Nobody here is saying anything. No paperwork for this one." Gretchen locked Lily and Ethan with a look that said, *I will eat you alive if you speak a word.* "And don't worry, we're not going to let Matthias get within an inch of you."

The others nodded as their signatures rose.

I forced a smile. Could we really stop Matthias? So far, he'd been able to operate with impunity. I knew we were lucky to have stopped him. That *I* was lucky not to be chained at his side.

Rhiannon's phone vibrated and she answered, mouthing to me, *I'll be right back. You okay?*

I nodded. Gretchen excused herself and started to tend to the wreckage of the prison, and the others followed. A few criminals had seemingly escaped, but soggy bluecoats were busy pulling them from the mud and dragging them back to confinement. Medics had arrived by transport charm and chopper and were tending to the wounded.

Spark scanned the prison grounds. *There are no hot dogs. No wonder no one wants to come here.* His eyes turned wistfully toward Exposition Park.

I laughed. "Go on, eat. You've earned it.

He cocked his head at me.

"Don't worry, I'm safe."

Spark stamped his feet. *I agree. Matthias will be brooding for a while. Call me if you need me. I will be hunting my favored prey.* He flapped his wings and rose into the air.

"Spark—"

He was gone, and a little pang of sadness washed over me.

I really hoped he wasn't going to rob Sammy's in dragon form. Spark would know better than to do that, right? He'd turn into a bobbing light. Or a mouse. Or something.

Probably?

I sighed. Worst-case scenario, I'd become persona non grata in Exposition Park. Best-case scenario, I was going to owe Sammy for a lot of Chicago dogs. Hopefully, the fates were on my side.

I ran my fingers through my hair. I was completely drained, and I sensed that it would be a long time before my strength returned. Perhaps days.

A wave of melancholy washed over me. I couldn't explain it, but somewhere deep inside, I knew that I would never wield power like that again. The power to banish a genie with a single word. The power to restore the ravages of time. It had been a gift of my transformation.

Though perhaps, I might feel a glimmer of it through a wish.

I released an exasperated sigh. I didn't understand my magic at all, and that terrified me more than Matthias or his genies did. When I'd wished to heal Damian, I'd seen a thousand possibilities. In the desperation of the moment, I'd randomly chosen one in which he was whole, but there had been many others.

Some of them dark.

I shuddered at how tempting those dark possibilities had been. What if I had chosen a different path?

I knew from the stories of genies that wishes had unintended consequences, often with disastrous ends. Could I really dance with the fates, or was I simply their puppet? What consequences had I already unleashed?

I shook the thoughts from my head. It didn't matter —I had Damian back.

It had been crystal-clear in the moment, and I had no doubt now that I couldn't live without him.

I turned back to him at last to tell him just that...

But Damian was gone.

Thanks for joining us on this adventure! If you've got an extra minute, please leave us a review on Amazon (http://mybook.to/Cursed-Angel). Reviews make a *huge* impact. They help us become better writers and keep us going through the difficult pages!

Are you ready for more? *Broken Skies*, the harrowing conclusion to the series, will be here in May 2021! You can pre-order here: hyperurl.co/brokenskies

Finally, if you'd like to chat more about the books, interact with fellow readers, and get the scoop on what's up next, join the Veronica Douglas Facebook group here:

https://www.facebook.com/groups/veronicadouglas

Thank you for reading *Cursed Angel*—we hope you enjoyed it as much as we did!

Magic Side is our little slice of Chicago. It's located on an island in Lake Michigan and is only visible to people with magic in their veins. The island's biggest and most famous park is Exposition Park, where Neve and Rhia like to grab a bite from Sammy's. The park is inspired by the real-life Jackson Park, which served as the site for the 1893 World's Columbian Exposition. It's our absolute favorite place to run in Chicago.

We've been fantasizing about doing fieldwork in Bulgaria and the Black Sea, so we decided to use them as a backdrop for a significant part of our book. The Bulgarian town of Sozopol is a real place located on the Black Sea coast. The town has a long and fascinating history and began as an ancient Greek trading colony in the 7th century BC. It later became known as Apollonia —presumably after the town's famous temple to Apollo, whose likely ruins are still visible today.

The island of Apollonia Parva, where Neve and Damian battle the hydra, is entirely fictional. Its inspiration came from St. Thomas Island, which is located about nine miles south of Sozopol. The island also has a colorful past, with remains spanning the Roman and Medieval periods. Curiously, the island is also known as Snake Island due to the water snakes that live in the waters around it.

Krasimir and his vampires actually have a historical precedent as well. Bulgaria was rife with vampirism in the Medieval period, and archaeologists have found dozens of graves where the remains were pierced through the chest with an iron or wooden bar. One of these skeletons was recently discovered in Sozopol, and was one of the main reasons we chose the town as a setting! Dubbed the vampire of Sozopol, he probably wasn't one of Kras's ancestors, but rather a very cruel nobleman named Krivich. When he died, the locals pierced his heart with an iron bar to ensure that he wouldn't rise again.

Cursed Angel is set in the wider Dragon's Gift universe created by Linsey Hall. We're huge fans of her writing and are super excited that we were able to weave Magic Side into her world. We started writing this series while Linsey was working on Shadow Guild: The Rebel, so Neve and Damian appear in the adventures of Grey and Carrow, as well as the adventures of Eve and Lachlan in Linsey's new series, Shadow Guild: Wolf Queen.

That's all for now but stay tuned for *Broken Skies*, the final book in Neve's series, which is coming out in May 2021. You can pre-order it here: hyperurl.co/brokenskies

Thank you again for reading, and be sure to sign up for our newsletter for sneak peaks, extra scenes, and super exclusive content! You can sign up at:

http://veronicadouglas.com/

BROKEN SKIES

DRAGON'S GIFT: THE STORM BOOK 4

VERONICA DOUGLAS
LINSEY HALL

I must risk everything.

I've become what I feared most, and a demon is hunting me for my power.

He's opened a portal to the underworld, and I'm the last piece in his puzzle. If he captures me, he'll use my magic to desolate the world.

The only person who can help me is Damian Malek, a cursed angel. He's sexy, powerful, and ruthless, and we can't seem to stay apart. The only problem is—our attraction is fatal.

When the veil to the underworld breaks, we've got one shot to save our world. We'll have to confront my past, find the secret of my magic, and broker a deal with the angels—a deal that could cost Damian everything.

Will it be enough, or will we both end up broken?

An action-packed urban fantasy, Broken Skies features a rebel heroine, a dark angel hero, and the spicy culmination of a slow burn romance. Prepare yourself for demons, shifters, and edge-of-your-seat adventure in the stunning finale of Dragon's Gift: The Storm.

If you enjoyed the archaeology, history, and daring in Linsey Hall's original Dragon's Gift books, this adventure is for you!
Pre Order: hyperurl.co/brokenskies

ACKNOWLEDGMENTS

VERONICA DOUGLAS

Thank you to everyone who has been so supportive, especially Lindsey and Ben—we love you guys!

Thank you to Jena O'Connor and Ash Fitzsimmons for your patience and amazing editing. We'd be nowhere with you.

Thank you to the amazing readers on our advanced review team! Special thanks to Susie, Penny, and Max for their suggestions and catches—you all are lifesavers!

And finally, a huge shoutout to Jes Ireland and Orina Kafe for the gorgeous cover art.

ACKNOWLEDGMENTS

LINSEY HALL

Thank you so much to Veronica and Doug, it's still so much fun to write with you guys!

And as usual, thank you to Ben. There would be no books without you.

Thank you to Jena O'Connor and Ash Fitzsimmons for your amazing editing. And to Jes Ireland and Orina Kafe for the beautiful cover.

ABOUT VERONICA DOUGLAS

Veronica Douglas is a duo of professional archaeologists that love writing and digging together. Veronica specializes in the archaeology of the early Islamic world, while Douglas studies ancient ships and Egypt. After spending an inordinate amount of time doing painstaking research for academia, they suddenly discovered a passion for letting their imaginations go wild! A cocktail of magic, romance, and ancient mystery (shaken, not stirred), their books are inspired, in part, by their life in Chicago and their archaeological adventures from around the globe.

ABOUT LINSEY HALL

Before becoming a writer, Linsey Hall was a nautical archaeologist who studied shipwrecks from Hawaii and the Yukon to the UK and the Mediterranean. She credits fantasy and historical romances with her love of history and her career as an archaeologist. After a decade of tromping around the globe in search of old bits of stuff that people left lying about, she settled down and started penning her own romance novels. Her series draw upon her love of history and the paranormal elements that she can't help but include.

Printed in Great Britain
by Amazon

62115041R00189